Just

ANOTHER DAY

at The Office

L. MOONE

CONTENTS

PART I.

I.

It's only nine-thirty am and already I can smell his armpits from across the large, shiny desk. What a complete creep! If I didn't need the money, I would've cut the interview short and made my escape by now…

How is he sweating so much? It's October, not mid-July!

My brain is on autopilot as he witters on about what he expects from me, I try to keep eye contact to a minimum while uttering generic responses where appropriate.

"Yes, I understand," I say.

Punctuality is important, got it. My eyes wander around the room, over the posed photographs of him sharing a handshake with some equally pompous looking dicks. Dick—an appropriate nickname for Richard Porter—purchasing manager at the largest electronic components distributor in West London, where I hope to be working soon.

By now I've seen enough of the over-dressed office from which he rules his domain and I stealthily glance through the window that overlooks the office floor. The desks are arranged in groups of three or four with low partition walls surrounding each cluster. All of the work areas that I can see are fully occupied except one.

"Yes, indeed I'm very excited to start my career here …" I hear myself say.

Just what the question was which prompted this response, I can't quite remember.

I give Richard—Dick—a quick glance. Pointless, he's still looking at my cleavage. Perhaps I should offer him a tissue. I shuffle uncomfortably in my seat. *Can I go now?*

Outside on the office floor the man who sits alone in a grouping of three desks catches my eye. He turns around in his chair as he answers the phone and only now can I fully appreciate him.

My age, or at the most thirty, if I had to guess. His full head of dark blond hair looks slightly longer than intended and somewhat messy. A perfect face, if there can be such a thing. Completely regular features and a straight nose as if copied from an ancient Greek statue; not that I recall seeing many Greek statues of a man of his build. Cuddly would be an appropriate descriptor.

I can't tell the exact colour of his eyes from here but even at this distance they express a certain kindness. He looks so serious, speaking into the phone with his full, sensual lips and a thoughtful look on his face.

I let my eyes travel down over his body—he's definitely a big guy, but it's hard to get a good look while he's sitting down. I can tell that he's straining against the white pinstriped shirt he's wearing. He should probably go a size up, not that I mind how it accentuates his dad bod.

I'd prefer the shirt off altogether.

He is so exactly my type, it's unnerving. My mind instantly conjures up images of him, on top of me, his broad arms cradling me as he leans in for a kiss. *Oh, what I could do to this man.*

"So, you'll handle a few easier accounts at first, then we'll re-evaluate, subject to successful completion of your three-month trial period," Dick says.

"Right," I answer. "Three months trial, okay."

I try to regain my composure, to hide the breathlessness I feel, but I can't take my eyes off my favorite future colleague. Will one of those empty desks become mine soon?

Suddenly, the fantasy disappears. The gorgeous face I was just admiring has twisted into an expression of shock, sadness. He's still on the phone, but he's stopped speaking. My heart starts beating even faster, only this time it's with concern. It's as though I can feel his pain from all the way over here.

I close my eyes for a moment and recover.

"So, who will I be working with?" I turn to Dick who is now finally looking up from my chest.

"You'll be working under Jonathan Hall, Senior Purchaser here at Aspect Technologies," he says as he motions over to the one occupied desk in a cluster of three, at my Mr. Perfect.

"Great, I guess I'll see you in two weeks then." I shake Dick's clammy hand as I get up.

Not certain how I should feel after all that, I take a few shaky steps toward the door. I've got the job. But what have I just witnessed out there?

As Dick walks me towards the elevator, I steal one last look at Jonathan. He is sitting completely still, staring at nothing while still holding the phone in mid-air. I try to give him a warm smile as I walk right through the path of his gaze, but he is completely oblivious.

I wish I could have overheard that phone call.

II.

For these past two weeks' time seemed to move at a crawl. The job promises to be the usual nine-to-five drudgery but I can hardly contain my excitement. The main reason of course is the prospect of working with Jonathan. Being able to make rent next month feels almost like a welcome bonus.

I wonder if my memory could be deceiving me. I suppose I'll find out soon enough if he really is everything I recall.

My buzzing phone brings me back to reality. A message from Jase:

Best of luck, girl. Go kick some arse!

It makes me smile. Of course he remembered that today is the day. I haven't been able to shut up about this job ever since the interview. Well, not about the job, but about the guy. Same thing really.

Thanks! x, I respond.

Now, what to wear… After pulling out nearly half the contents of my wardrobe and dumping them on the bed I settle on a slightly-too-tight plum pencil skirt and a black cowl-neck pullover. A tad more conservative than my usual style, but I wouldn't want to fall foul of any yet to be discovered dress code. At least the pullover makes the outfit somewhat appropriate for the blustery weather that's typical for London in late October.

Plus, there's still that sleazy creep, Dick Porter, to contend with. A pair of back seamed stockings and heels should do nicely to keep things interesting.

Dress to impress.

I'm fifteen minutes early coming out of the lift at my new workplace. Most of the desks are still empty, as is the office in the corner. I'm guessing Dick doesn't take punctuality to extremes himself. *Good.*

I hesitate and look around for any familiar faces. Dick's assistant, Sharon, is just now walking into the office as well. She is quite imposing, a bit taller than me with a slightly heavier, more curvaceous build, as well as impeccable dress sense. Her demeanour suggests she takes herself a bit too seriously. I don't want to judge too quickly though, so I put on my friendliest smile.

"Morning, I'm Cath. We met two weeks ago when I came in for my interview. Today is my first day..."

"Oh yes, Catherine. Richard isn't in yet; he'll be here at nine. Why don't you take a seat over there—" She gestures towards the right side of the office where I already expected to be sitting, "—and make yourself comfortable."

Her tone is authoritative. She's used to being in charge.

"Thanks," I mutter, while anxiously scanning the office for Jonathan.

There is a backpack lying on what I remember to be his desk, but he's not around. So I put my stuff on the empty desk right next to his and sit down to wait. Nervous doesn't quite describe how I feel.

"Hi." His baritone voice behind me makes me jump up instantly. It sounds pleasantly warm but slightly raspy, as though he's fighting a cold.

"Err, hi. I'm Cath—short for Catherine but nobody actually calls me that. They tell me I'm going to be working with you…" And now I'm rambling. *Great.*

I look at his face while offering my hand to greet him formally. Gorgeous as I remembered. But in spite of the proverbial rose-tinted specs which are currently clouding my vision, I can't help but notice a difference about him.

Are those dark circles I'm seeing? Even his skin tone has changed from the healthy subtle tan I remember to ashen and dull. I fight the urge to stare. My fingers itch to reach up and touch his face, but of course I do nothing of the sort.

"Yes indeed. Morning. I'm John," he says as we shake hands. His hand is slightly colder than mine but his grip is strong. It takes a lot of willpower for me to let go.

Holding my breath, I fight my nerves to look into his eyes momentarily. They're a warm shade of amber, but at the same time they betray more than the rest of his appearance has already done. Tired and empty. I'm taken aback by what I see and quickly look away again.

I dare not stare or make eye contact again all morning while he is giving me an introduction to all the systems I'm supposed to be using. There's no hint of small talk, only work. Even then, he appears to be a man of few words.

Whenever I do glance at his face, I notice he's consistently avoiding the sight of me. If he's not looking at the computer screen, he's leafing through the mountain of papers on his desk. Now I'm not expecting every man to act like Dick *'Pervert' 'Porter* and shamelessly ogle my boobs all day. But to avoid looking in my direction completely is another unusual extreme.

And it's especially frustrating, because I desperately wish for John to notice me.

While he busies himself with some papers in the filing cabinet behind his desk, I allow my eyes to linger on him for a moment.

Ever since I can remember I've liked men with a bit of meat on them. I don't quite understand it—I don't have any identifiable reason for this preference. I've long given up trying to analyse myself. All I know is, I want to feel his soft skin under my fingertips. I want his belly brushing against me as he leans down for a kiss. *I want...*

"Cath, was it?" says a familiar voice behind me. "How are you enjoying your first day?"

Dick. His presence makes the hairs on the back of my neck stand up, and not in a good way. The inappropriate fantasy that had started to play out in my mind is instantly shattered.

"Great," I say. "There's so much to learn, but John has been really patient with me."

"Good, good. Carry on!" I can hardly suppress a sigh of relief as he stalks off towards another cluster of desks.

I turn to face John. "What time is lunch?"

"Ten minutes."

***

The lunchroom is spacious and bright. There is a buffet of sandwiches on offer and a suspicious looking "Soup of the day". I buy a ham and cheese sandwich and join a group of about seven women who are already eating and chatting at one of the two large tables.

There's no sign of John.

"Hi, I'm Cath. I've just started today," I introduce myself as the others give me the visual once-over. The only one I've already met is Sharon, who gestures at the empty seat next to her.

"Catherine, join us. I'll introduce everyone." She's smiling at me but her eyes don't look friendly.

Maybe my first impression was somewhat correct after all: she seems to be in charge. Or at least she thinks she is.

Sharon quickly rattles through the names of everyone at the table.

"This is Linda, Shelley, Jessica, Amanda, Heidi and Jackie." I nod at each of them before taking a seat.

"So, Cath. How do you like Aspect so far?" a woman further along the table asks.

Amanda, I think, but I'm not entirely sure. Her smile seems more genuine than Sharon's, but perhaps she's just a better actress.

"Oh, it seems like a nice place to work. Of course, I'm just overwhelmed at all the new things I'm supposed to learn."

"Right. So, you've been paired with John," she says. Her voice sounds awkward as she speaks his name. "How's *that* going?"

"Fine… He seems knowledgeable," I say.

"He should be. It seems like he's always here; comes in early and leaves late. Well he used to anyway. We've been wondering if he secretly has a bed hidden away in the supply cupboard," one of the others butts in.

The group laughs in response.

I smile politely at their rather sad attempt at a joke, and eat my food. The conversation moves on to other topics, mainly reality TV. *The X Factor* and *Strictly Come Dancing*. I don't watch either, so have nothing much to contribute.

* John *

Bloody great.

First Julie puts me through hell, and now that moron Richard is having me train his insufferable new recruit. The fun just keeps piling up, threatening to claim what's left of my sanity.

I caught a glimpse of her from behind as she arrived for her interview. Exactly Richard's type. Long legs leading up to probably the greatest ass ever to have set foot in this building. She'll fit right in with Sharon and her gang, so why couldn't one of them train her?

It's obvious why he hired her; and previous experience clearly wasn't a deciding factor.

This whole thing must be his idea of a joke. The way

he looked at her when he came over to say hello… disgusting.

It'll be a few days before he makes his move. She will most definitely go for it too. They usually do.

I hadn't even seen her up close until this morning. She's his ultimate checklist personified: gorgeous figure with curves in just the right places, well dressed, and young. And her face…

I am not the type of guy who tends to objectify women, far from it. But this one—I can't even look at her without having to fight one physical reaction or another.

Best to ignore her completely. Once I get this training over with, everything can go back to normal.

A glance at my watch tells me it's time. Back to the grind…

I quickly hide the bottle of vodka behind the stack of spare copier paper. I don't know why I bother with this anymore. It doesn't even help.

When I get to my desk she is already sitting at her computer, peering at the screen with intense focus. I sit down and retrieve the sheet with today's training topics from the mess on my desk. The letters are blurring a little, but I'm sure I can bluff my way through. After all, she doesn't know anything yet.

Here goes nothing…

"Let's continue, shall we?" I say, wishing for the day to just end already.

III.

I am rudely awakened by the sound of my alarm.

The leftovers of the delicious dream I've been having still linger, confusing me. John was in it, of course. I can't quite recall much else, but my ragged breath and moist, tingly crotch suggest that we weren't getting much work done.

As I get ready and head into work, I can't stop obsessing about what's been going on lately.

Despite working with John for a few days already, I really can't seem to get a read on him. All my efforts to start a conversation have stumbled at the first hurdle.

I do wonder, is he always like this? Or perhaps he genuinely dislikes me? Although I keep going through whatever I've done or said, and I can't pinpoint anything specific that might have caused this rift.

I haven't even had the chance to say anything too daft yet. We haven't had a single conversation that wasn't about work.

Today, I think I'll have lunch with the girls again. Perhaps they have some insights to share.

By the time I reach the office and make my way towards my desk, John is already there for a change. Normally he's nowhere to be seen until nine am sharp.

And he looks even bleaker than on Monday.

Something is definitely wrong with him. Perhaps that's the reason he isn't talking.

Whatever it is, I'll be the last person he'll open up to. He seems to be the sort of guy to bottle everything up.

Speaking of bottles, I'm convinced he has a stash somewhere around the office. Every lunch hour he sneaks off and comes back with a distinct smell hanging around him. They say vodka doesn't make your breath smell, but that's untrue.

It's only a matter of time before someone catches on, even if I'm the only one who appears to be paying attention. Maybe I should say something? But considering he hates me, I don't think it'll go down well.

"So, what's the plan for today?" I say, forcing myself to look him right in the face this time.

I've been practising but my heart still skips a few beats every time I do. How does he not notice or care just how nervous he makes me?

John is just sitting there, fingertips rubbing his temples and eyes closed in a frown. Hangover? Time to take some initiative.

"I'm going to get myself a cuppa, would you like anything?" I try again. Nothing.

I shrug and head to the hot drinks machine. *Fine, I'll improvise.* When I get back to our desks, he's still sitting in the same position.

"Here, have some tea. You look like you need it." I push one of the two paper cups towards him, as well as a couple of sugar packets and a wooden stirrer.

"I wasn't sure how you take it."

Finally, he looks up at me and I just about manage to hide my nerves with a friendly expression. I hope.

"Thanks," he says, and our eyes meet for but a split second.

I quickly look away and fidget with my own ribbed cardboard cup before taking a sip.

As my heart rate comes down, I can't help but smile into my drink.

There's something pure about tea. How it can turn almost any situation right around.

When I glance over at John, he's just brought his cup to his lips. His face has straightened out and he looks a bit more relaxed than he has done all of this week. As soon as I focus on my cup again, I feel his eyes on me and I can hardly suppress another smile.

This morning, the training goes a little better than it has so far. Either I'm starting to pick things up, or he's become more patient. He's even speaking in complete sentences rather than monosyllabic words.

Whatever the cause, I'm encouraged by the results.

"Say, have you heard about the old cinema in Kingston; I heard they did a brilliant job on the renovations. It feels like forever since I've been to the movies…" I try, hoping to steer the conversation away from work.

"Yeah, the opening was what, last weekend? I haven't been yet," he answers.

An actual chat, even if it was just one exchange— amazing what a cup of tea can do!

"Lunchtime. See you after," he says while getting up.

I still haven't seen him set foot in the lunchroom even once. I wonder where he goes every day?

"Later," I respond.

When I enter the break area, the conversation at the lunch table is already in full swing.

"Hi, Cath, join us!" Amanda waves at me. During the few times we've shared lunch, she has been the nicest to me out of the whole group.

I sit down next to her and start listening in. There's some event coming up and everyone is buzzing.

"I overheard Richard the other day talking to upper management. Apparently it will be black tie this year! And everyone's allowed a plus-one, not like our usual parties," Amanda continues. Her voice is shrill with excitement.

They can only be talking about the obligatory office Christmas party. I'm not sure whether to look forward to it or dread the entire affair.

Bring a date? The only date I want sits next to me every day… But what if he has someone already? I don't have a clue about his personal life.

"So, when is this thing happening?" I ask casually.

"Saturday, December 1st. I'm sure they'll send out a circular shortly," Amanda says.

That gives me—let's see—just about four weeks.

The conversation moves on. Dick allegedly hooked up with some girl in Finance. I feel sorry for her, but my sentiments aren't shared by the rest of the group, it seems.

Half of them decide to leave early, preparing for some meeting I'm not privy to. I get a moment alone with Amanda and decide to make the most of it.

"Say, I've been wondering. Is John always this grumpy or have I done something to cause it?" I ask.

"Well..." Her voice lowers. "Actually, no. I mean, he's never been very chatty, but lately—I probably shouldn't say anything."

Please, please do tell! I try not to look too eager, but can't keep my eyes off her in anticipation of what she's about to share.

She takes a deep breath before continuing in a low whisper. "A few weeks ago, he broke up with his girlfriend."

"Really!" I raise my eyebrows.

"Yeah, it was messy, too. I don't know why, but for some reason she called the office and not his mobile. All calls reach Linda's line first and then she transfers them. So, she transferred the call to John but—" Amanda hesitates and scans the empty room.

"She never hung up. Heard the whole thing."

My mind is racing. This must have been the phone call I witnessed during my job interview.

The sneaking off, the drinking at lunchtime… It all starts to make sense now.

I can't believe Linda would do such a thing! Okay, that's not true. I have no trouble believing it at all.

"Oh my, and she told everyone what she overheard?" I ask.

"Yeah. I mean, I'm not really friendly with him, but that was quite a crappy thing to do. The girl told him she had never really been into him, that she had just needed a place to stay for free. She really tore him down, it was really cruel." Amanda shakes her head.

My mouth has fallen wide open. I'm torn between sadness and outrage.

"Unbelievable," I mutter.

As I wander towards my desk, my mind is still racing to process this new information. So, he is indeed single, but the circumstances make me feel guilty for hoping so earlier on.

My heart aches for him, but what can I do about it? If he gets the feeling that I'm only being nice to him out of pity, that would make everything worse.

That's not how things are, anyway.

He mustn't find out that I know. Ever.

"Hi." I smile and make proper eye contact for the first time in quite a while.

My heart skips a whole bunch of beats, yet my eyes linger on his just a little longer.

"Hey. Ready to be introduced to some suppliers?" he asks.

Do my ears deceive me or is his voice just a little more upbeat than normal?

"Yeah, but I could really use a bit of caffeine first— shall I get you one too?" I ask.

"Sure, thanks." A reluctant smile appears.

I guess the saying is true: the way to a man's heart is through his stomach. I sure as hell can play that game! Off I go, with a spring in my step.

The hot drinks machine is in the hallway just around the corner, opposite the lifts. It's quiet at this time of day, allowing me to plot my next move. I must get him to open up more.

Just when I'm picking up the two cups to head back to my desk, I start to feel uneasy. It's as though I can feel someone's presence nearby.

"Hi, Cath—getting a cup of tea, I see?" Dick appears right behind me.

I must have been so lost in my thoughts that I didn't notice him walking over.

"Um, yeah. Nothing like some caffeine to increase productivity..." I respond with a flat smile.

He's standing way too close for comfort. Has the man never heard of personal space?

"Good, good. I won't keep you. I was just wondering..." He leans closer, with one hand against the drinks machine, blocking my way. "Perhaps you'd like to join me for drinks sometime? We could go somewhere after work."

Wait, didn't he already get with some woman from Finance recently?I shudder at the thought.

"Thanks, but I don't think that's a good idea," I mumble.

My eyes are now scanning around the empty hallway, hoping for someone to walk in and distract him. Thankfully, a moment later Sharon appears and I don't hesitate to seize my chance.

"Oh, Sharon, good thing you're here. I was wondering—" I quickly duck underneath Dick's arm and get a few paces between us. "Where is the extra sugar kept? The dispenser here is almost out."

Sharon looks at me, frowning, then looks back at

Dick, who is still standing by the machine.

"Oh, that's okay, I'll take care of it." Sharon continues to look at us with a suspicious scowl on her face.

"Great, thanks. Back to work," I mutter while hurrying back into the office floor.

Hopefully Dick gets the message that I'm not interested, but something tells me he isn't the type to quit easily.

* John *

Today went a lot better than expected, despite my epic hangover this morning.

The new girl, Cath, is really trying to be friendly. Maybe she's not just a pretty face; she seems to be unlike the others: actually nice.

She went to get a cup of tea after lunch and came back looking flustered. When I asked what was wrong, she wasn't forthcoming. The only hint she gave was when she asked about Richard in a roundabout fashion. *What's his deal?* That's literally what she said.

I had to assume he tried some of his so-called charms on her—that's what he always does. And apparently it didn't work.

For some reason this really cheered me up. While Sharon and the others continue to suck up to him all day, she's not interested.

I thought I was the only one who saw him for the despicable arse that he is. She was being careful not to say anything too incriminating, of course. But I could tell from how she said his name that she's not a fan.

After finishing for the day, we got talking a little. She said she likes to know the people she works with, something to that effect. We talked about silly stuff mostly—movies, music, that sort of thing. It turns out she's unusual indeed, in fact we share very similar tastes.

It was nice. A little conversation about nothing, really. She's excited about the final season of *Game of Thrones*, but said her benchmark epic fantasy will always remain *The Lord of the Rings*.

I would have never taken her for a Tolkien nerd. Interesting.

When she got up to leave, she casually touched my arm while saying goodbye. My skin is still buzzing in that spot even now. I hope she didn't notice if I acted weird. It's just a casual gesture, she wouldn't have meant anything by it…

"Yeah, I'll have another. Double," I say, while brushing my hand over that spot on my arm. It's as though I can still feel her touch.

The young woman behind the bar has given up on taking my empty glasses away, instead opting to simply refill them. I don't know how many times. The whisky has stopped burning on my tongue, so I must've had a few already.

But why can't I get her out of my head? If only she knew the effect she's having on me, she'd dislike me just like she does Richard.

Still, she's all I can think about.

IV.

"Morning, John," I say when I reach our desks, tea in hand.

When I initially came in, he was here already in much the same condition as yesterday, so I headed for the hot drinks machine straight away. Perhaps this is going to turn into a ritual of sorts.

He takes the cup, giving me an apologetic smile.

"Rough night?" I guess that wasn't really a question.

He responds with an unintelligible noise rather than actual words.

"I wish you'd take it easy on yourself." Shit, did I actually just say that?

He instantly looks up in surprise. I wish the earth would swallow me whole, but here I am. All I can do to deflect is to fidget with my cup some more.

Shut up, woman! The last thing I want is to remind him of his mom.

"Anyway..." I say, in a desperate attempt to fill the awkward silence. "I hope you like chocolate chip."

He doesn't hesitate to help himself to the open biscuit packet I'm holding in his direction.

We're both quiet again, eating and drinking our tea. I've always been clumsy, so it's no surprise I'm spilling crumbs all over the front of my dress. I casually try and brush them off, when I notice Dick leaning against the door frame leading to his office, watching me.

There is something so creepy in his stare; it puts me off immediately.

"Erm, John… " I clear my throat, and lean across just low enough to get out of Dick's line of sight. "I hope you don't mind but I would like to ask a favor."

"Yeah, sure. What is it?" he says.

"Well, you know the other day I asked about D… erm, Richard?" I start.

"Yeah…"

"It's just—he's been acting funny." I take a deep breath. *Better out than in!* I might as well figure out where he stands.

"Well he's giving me weird vibes. Would you mind— you know—sort of hanging around when he comes over? I'd rather not be alone with the guy."

My heart is pounding in my chest. I thought I could tell that he didn't like Dick either when we talked about him yesterday. Hopefully it wasn't a trick!

"Uh, sure…" He smiles at me.

I guess he does understand. *Thank God!*

When I straighten myself, I can't see Dick anymore; perhaps he's wandered off to be creepy someplace else.

It seems that John thinks I've learnt quite enough for the time being, so he gives me a few jobs to do on my own and the morning passes without further excitement. I decide to have my packed lunch at my desk today.

As usual John is away for the whole hour. I thought I saw him go into the copier room, but surely he can't have stayed in there the whole time? I must have just missed him leaving.

Dick is apparently busy with meetings all afternoon, which doesn't surprise me. That's what management jobs seem to be all about. In any case it's a good thing because I don't risk running into him.

By five o'clock he's back though, lurking around his office, and stealing glances in my direction. John is getting ready to leave for the day, so I don't have much time to spare.

"Umm, John, mind if I walk down with you?" I say.

He throws a quick glance in Dick's direction, before looking back at me.

"Yeah, no problem. I'll wait."

I give him a grateful smile and quickly pack up my bag.

Unfortunately, the way out is right past Dick's office, and as we walk by I hear him clearing his throat.

"Cath. Have you got a minute?" Dick asks.

He shoots a suspicious look at John, but the latter doesn't move from my side. My knight in shining armour!

"Oh, Richard, I'm sorry I have to hurry, doctor's appointment. I hope whatever it is can wait until Monday?" I respond with a fake smile.

Dick doesn't look pleased but waves me on.

"Yeah, no problem. Have a good weekend, then."

John and I briskly walk out into the hallway and to the lifts.

"Doctor's appointment, eh?" He grins at me.

"Well. I figured that would be hard to argue with." I

smile back at him.

The lift doors close behind us. Alone with him in this small space, my heart starts racing even more. If this were a RomCom, one of us would make their first move right about now.

The near mirror finish of the doors allows me to keep stealing glances at John's reflection. I don't think he notices, at least I hope not. He looks as though he's quite lost in thoughts.

Unfortunately, life isn't a movie. Too soon, the doors open again.

"Well, goodnight. Have a nice weekend!" I say, suppressing a sigh as I put my hand on his arm in sort of a goodbye gesture. I don't want to let go.

"Thanks, see you on Monday." His voice sounds flatter than usual, but I'm probably just projecting my own feelings onto him. I wish I would see him sooner than that.

✳✳✳

With nothing going on, my weekend is promising to be excruciatingly boring.

I phone up Jase on Saturday morning for some 'girl talk' and hopefully some insight into the male psyche. I've always been able to rely on him to help me through my dating dilemmas in the past. Though ever since he moved to Edinburgh, it's been harder for us to really connect.

"Hey there, darling, what's going on?" he asks.

It's good to hear his voice after all these days. I've

missed him.

"Oh, you know. Same old, pretty much. You know I've been having so much trouble getting John to notice me, but it seems offering hot drinks and food has helped a bit."

Jase laughs at the other end. "He's a man! What did you expect? Warm him up with food, followed up by a revealing outfit. I'm sure you can figure it out."

I sigh.

"Well that's exactly the problem. God knows I've been trying to dress for success, so to speak. Unfortunately, it hasn't had any effect. In the meantime, I'm having issues keeping my sleazy boss at arm's length. It seems he's under the impression I'm trying to send *him* the signals, if you know what I mean."

"Okay, that's odd. You're definitely on the right track, but John just isn't paying attention, then? You sure he doesn't play for my team?"

"Well, I heard he had a girlfriend, but they split up recently. So I'd say it's unlikely," I answer.

"So, that's the issue. The poor boy is heartbroken! Give him time. Or if you get too impatient, you'll have to hit him over the head with a stack of papers before dragging him home with you. That'll make him take notice." Jase chuckles to himself.

I roll my eyes. Jason has no idea what it's like to be shy.

"Yeah, I guess you're right. I need to be more patient. Well, anyway, I'm going to have a little think about what to do. At least I got him talking a little bit last week," I say.

"Don't worry, sooner or later he'll come around. He'd be an idiot not to," he reassures me.

"Thanks. Where would I be without you and your wonderful insights into the world of men?"

I sigh.

"No problem, love. Hey, I gotta head to the salon. Call me back at night if you wanna talk some more," he responds.

"Sure. Later."

I hang up the phone.

Our chat has made me feel a bit better. Maybe John would like to just be friends, at least for a while until he sorts himself out?

Wonder what's on TV...

V.

Before I know it, the week of the Christmas bash is upon us and I'm no closer to asking John to be my date. I could pretend that I prefer the man to make the first move because I'm old-fashioned like that. But really, I'm too terrified to put myself out there.

What if he says no?

After talking it out with Jason a few more times, I did decide to at least obtain an outfit for the night. As boring as it was to go shopping by myself, his expert advice was only a phone call away. Sending him pictures of the various options from the changing room almost made me feel like he was with me, just like the old days before life moved us apart.

I really need some more people in my life who don't live on the other end of the country.

I'm at my desk at nine sharp and immediately notice some paperwork I'd forgotten about in my hurry on Friday. I was supposed to make copies! Quickly, I dump my bag on the floor and gather up all the required documents.

I burst through the door leading into the copier room and am greeted by an unexpected sight. John mutters some curse words under his breath, while furiously trying to hide something behind the spare paper.

Our eyes meet and I can see the embarrassment

written all over him. My gaze is drawn to the reams of paper behind him, but I don't even need to see it. I have a pretty good guess what it is already.

So, we've moved beyond lunchtime drinks and on to breakfast ones? I don't approve, but who am I to get involved?

"Relax, I won't tell," I break the silence.

He doesn't speak.

"I just needed to copy these… Totally forgot on Friday." I hold up the stack of documents in my hands.

He still looks embarrassed.

Awkward.

"Really, I don't care! I mean I do care, but what you do is your business," I add. "Plus, you already know how much I love talking to Richard. You're quite safe, alright?"

John gives me a grateful look and takes a couple of steps towards me and the copier.

"Here, let me show you how to use this thing," he says.

I'm perfectly capable of operating a copier myself, but I don't protest. Instead, I stand by and enjoy being in close proximity to him while he does it for me.

I really wish he would talk about what he's going through. Surely that would be better than how he's been handling it so far? But it's too much to expect, I know that. We're only barely past the 'What's your favourite song?' stage.

We get back to our desks and sit down shortly after. I rummage around in my bag until I find what I'm looking for.

"Here, I don't want you getting caught." I hand him the packet of gum.

"Oh, thanks." His eyes are fixated on the gum for a moment. His frown suggests that he's trying to think of something more to say. Nothing follows and I decide to let it go.

All morning he is even more preoccupied than usual. And for that matter, so am I. After Friday's quick getaway, I'm fully expecting Dick to make another attempt at whatever he was trying to do that evening.

Finally, my paranoia reaches record highs and I simply have to ask John. "Say, have you seen Richard around today?"

"Oh, you didn't know? He's gone on a business trip. Won't be back until Friday evening."

I breathe a sigh of relief.

"Well, thank fuck for that." I cover my mouth and glance at him to gauge his reaction. "Sorry. That was inappropriate."

This little exchange seems to have amused John, who leans back in his chair and looks at me for a moment.

"Why don't you just tell him you've got a boyfriend and you're not interested?"

"I'm a terrible liar. About the boyfriend, I mean. Just telling him I wasn't interested didn't have much effect," I respond.

He slowly shakes his head while scrutinising me with one eyebrow raised.

"What?" I ask.

"A girlfriend, then?" he continues.

"Nope. Just me for the past year or so," I respond.

Finally, a personal conversation. This is my opening! "How about you?"

"Oh." He hesitates. "Not anymore."

"I'm sorry." I decide to try my luck and probe further. "What happened?"

I immediately regret asking, it's bad enough everyone else found out thanks to Linda's idiotic behaviour.

"Just didn't work out." He shrugs. There's a blank look in his eyes.

"Yeah, I know what you mean." My poor attempt at showing solidarity hits a wall. Rightly so.

There is no more meaningful conversation until we say our goodbyes for the day.

***

It's Tuesday morning, and John is nowhere to be seen. Perhaps he's called in sick? I wonder if he's feeling uneasy after I walked in on him yesterday in the copier room? Or perhaps my attempted interrogation regarding his personal life put him off?

Maybe I'm reading too much into this; he could just have a plain old cold. It's been doing the rounds in the office ever since winter set in properly.

There is plenty for me to do all day, now that I'm supposedly through my basic training, so I try not to think about it too much.

Wednesday and Thursday pass in a similar fashion. I grow more concerned though, wondering if John is okay. Whether he is indeed sick, or maybe just busy drinking himself into oblivion? Either way, it's not a good thought.

So naturally I feel a huge sense of relief on Friday morning when I see him come in.

"Morning, John! Are you alright?" I greet him.

He is in quite a state, but it's hard to tell whether it's due to flu or if he's just massively hungover again. He doesn't say anything, just sits down.

I fetch us some tea and decide to wait and see, but there isn't much change in him.

Suddenly he gets up and heads to another door leading off from our office, the store room. I wait for a while, but he doesn't return. After ten minutes or so I can't fight my impatience anymore and decide to check in.

"John?" I call him softly, opening the door to the store room. No answer, but I see him standing completely still in the corner, staring at the wall. *What is he doing in there?*

I close the door behind me and move towards him.

"Are you alright?" I ask.

He looks at me, barely. His eyes are red and puffy. "Julie... and my brother—"

He shuts his eyes and slowly shakes his head.

Julie, is that his ex? *Oh dear, this can't be good.*

I put my hand on his arm. "Tell me what happened."

"That fucking bastard..." His breaths are strained. He tries to compose himself before continuing. "I decided to take a couple of days and check in on my folks this week. My brother still lives at home with them…"

I take his hand and squeeze it gently, encouraging him to keep talking. No reaction. At least he doesn't pull it away.

"They weren't home at the time, but *she* was there, Cath. I saw her and Dan, in his room. Oh God." His voice reduces to a whisper as he tells me the story.

This makes it all so much worse; first the break-up phone call becoming public knowledge at work, and now his ex has decided to move on to his brother. Who knows how long *that* has been going on for?

"Shit, John. That's horrible!" I say.

"And the worst part is, I'm not even fucking surprised. It still hurts, though!" He awkwardly looks down at my hand, still holding his. My heart is racing so hard, I can't help but wonder if he can sense it.

I so badly want to hold him, make all of this go away. But I have to remind myself not to be so bloody selfish. This isn't about me and what I want. He's obviously still hung up on her.

"I know it probably won't help, but I do know what it's like to be betrayed. What a shitty thing for them to do. You deserve way better!" I grab a roll of kitchen towel off the shelf next to me and hand him a sheet.

"It'll be okay, you know. You won't feel like this forever." I watch him as he takes the paper towel and dabs his eyes.

"If you want to go home or something, I'll cover for you. In any case, Richard isn't around."

He shakes his head. "Thanks, but I've got work to do."

We walk out of the store room one after the other. Luckily the office is very quiet this morning and we're not observed.

Almost straight away we get started with our work, pretending nothing has happened. But I still can't shake the urge to do something—anything—to try and reach out.

At lunchtime we fall into our usual routines. He's off *'copying'*, while I stay at my desk with the sandwich I carried from home.

Ill-advised though it may be, I tear a sheet off my notepad and start scribbling.

'Any time you want to talk,' I write, putting my phone number and address underneath.

I tuck it into the front pocket of his bag, where he keeps his keys. Foolish maybe, but I really had to do something.

From all our previous conversations I gathered we're quite similar; he also doesn't have many friends. At least I still have Jase, who is only a phone call away. Everyone needs someone to confide in, surely?

Might as well be me.

VI.

I'm half-asleep on the sofa, and no longer really registering the blue flicker of the TV, when I hear the doorbell. I glance at the clock—one am. Who could be at the door in the middle of the bloody night?

I jump up and smooth down my hair as best I can, but I know I look exactly like I feel; like I've just woken up.

Well, tough. Whoever is here will just have to deal with it.

I open the door slightly with the chain on, and catch a glimpse of John. I immediately close the door again to take off the chain, then open it wide to let him in. He looks even more troubled than usual, and the smell of booze hangs heavy in the air.

"What the fuck, Cath!" He's slurring his words. "Why? Why do you toy with me?"

"Whoa. Not sure what you're talking about, John." I step back and watch as he comes in.

He staggers into the kitchenette and leans on the counter, his head hanging low.

Am I dreaming? Is he even really here? Is it wise to let him into my place like this?

"What do you mean, toy with you?" I ask, rubbing my eyes.

"You know, acting so damn nice all the time. If I didn't know any better, I'd think you were dropping hints. You think I'd fall for it? And then you leave me this—" He shows me the crumpled-up piece of paper in his hand. The note I'd left in his bag earlier that day.

Oh shit.

"Fall for what?" I ask, while placing my hand against his arm in an attempt to calm him down.

Instead, he flinches as soon as I touch him.

"This! What the fuck is this?" He gestures down at my hand, then looks at me. His expression is wild.

I ought to back away in fear. This could turn out to be a huge mistake. It's not anger I see in his eyes, it's something else. I'm not afraid.

"It might not be a big deal to you, just a gesture, but don't you understand? This drives me crazy!" he rants.

Finally, it dawns on me what he's trying to say.

"Oh, but it is a big deal to me," I whisper. "I don't go around putting my hands on all and sundry. Especially not at the office."

"And I know that, sooner or later, when I can't take it anymore, and I want more," he continues to ramble. "It'll be like I'm fucking fifteen all over again. If you are actually as nice as you pretend to be, you'll let me down easy—say you just wanna be friends..."

He looks down at the floor again, but I can see tears in his eyes.

I can't believe it—he actually likes me that way! All this time it had felt like I was talking to a wall, like nothing I did could make him notice me as anything other than a colleague. But he *did* notice, and he misunderstood every last signal I was trying to send.

"John," I say, while cupping his face. "You don't understand."

I can feel tears welling up in my eyes too, but his gaze evades mine. I stand on tiptoe so our eyes are only inches apart now.

"I do not want to be *just friends*. I've had a crush on you since I first saw you..."

His eyes widen in disbelief, and our lips meet in a near perfect first kiss.

Hesitant and gentle, his lips press so softly against mine it makes me ache for more. A tear escapes my eye and rolls down my cheek.

I drink in his scent. Although it's masked by how much he's had to drink tonight; I can still taste *him* through it all. My hands have moved on, fingers running through his hair and pulling him down into me. He is starting to react, returning my kisses, until we're both equally breathless. I coax his lips apart some more, allowing my tongue to find his, dancing around it.

When our tongues finally meet, it's as if the floodgates open inside of me, releasing all the desire I had locked up inside all these weeks. Blood rushes outwards from my core into the farthest parts of my body until even my fingertips are buzzing with excitement.

His large, strong hands find their way onto my back. He holds me so tightly against him. I can feel his warm body crushing against me and it drives me wild with desire. I've dreamt of this moment so many times and it does not disappoint.

I take a step back, and he abruptly releases me.

"I'm sorry, I didn't mean to..." he stammers.

I shake my head and smile, and lead him by the hand towards the sofa. If this is a dream, it's the best I've ever had.

"I'm not sorry," I say, before pushing him down. "I've been wanting to do this for so long..."

His eyes widen with surprise as I kneel beside him on the sofa, and lean in for another kiss. The excitement inside me is growing with every shallow breath I take and I can tell I'm having a similar effect on him. I keep losing myself in the moment. The only thing reminding me this isn't just a dream is that, when I manage to open my eyes every so often, I see his face right in front of mine. He's exactly where I want him to be, finally.

Unbelievable.

His eyes seem to be losing focus, as though the long day as well as the drink is catching up with him. This isn't fair for either of us, so I pull away just slightly.

"You look tired," I remark, while tracing the dark lines under his eyes with my fingertips.

"Here." I hand him the forgotten glass of water that has been sitting on the coffee table for the better part of the evening.

While watching him drink, and in spite of the fire he stirred in me I can feel how exhausted I am myself. It's the middle of the night after all.

But he's here now.

We have nothing but time. I'd rather he sobers up before we do anything else.

VII. JOHN

I'm dizzy, like the world underneath me is moving. Side to side a few times, I shift myself to get more comfortable and the movement stops.

In my dream, I'm surrounded by strange noises. Footsteps, rustling sounds and running water. My mind is still foggy and my eyelids remain heavy and stubborn. I don't want to face reality yet.

A loud click startles me fully awake—was that a door? I blink a few times before the room comes into focus.

This place does not look familiar at all. A TV, Xbox and a stack of DVDs at eye level in a dark wood finish cabinet with a bunch of black candles in a holder on top. This is definitely someone's living room, but whose? And how did I get here? I try to move, but my head feels like it's made of lead.

The candles are odd—who would have candles in their living room? *Oh shit, is this a girl's house?* This possibility seems implausible, and yet as I stretch a bit and look around, I can see more evidence to support it. A purple hair band lying on the coffee table in front of me. It matches the curtains. It even smells of girl in here, flowery and sweet, like a very light perfume.

Carefully I try and sit up, worried that any sudden movement might have unwanted consequences.

Where the fuck am I? What happened last night?

I remember the pub, but my memory gets hazy after I ordered some chicken wings quite a few drinks into the evening. I've really overdone it this time. Never before have I blacked out like this.

Looking at the coffee table again, I'm starting to panic. It seems I'm alone here, and it still escapes me whose house it could be. I don't recall even talking to another soul at the pub, other than to place my orders.

For what feels like forever, I just sit there on the couch with my head in my hands trying to figure out what's going on. Wish it would stop hurting already so I could focus.

This entire scenario isn't just unlikely, it seems impossible. Wouldn't I have remembered it if I went home with someone?

I look down at myself, still wearing the same office clothes, though my shirt is untucked and belt loosened. No idea where my shoes are and how this fluffy blanket got around me.

All of this is too confusing. If by some sort of cosmic accident, I managed to chat up a woman and convince her to let me into her home... If anything like that happened, then why am I on the couch and not in a bed? And if I just passed out here, then where did *she* go? Maybe she's uncomfortable with my presence and hopes that I'll leave before she gets back. That part would make sense.

I'm straining to get up, when all my body wants to do is lie back down. The armrest of the sofa is the only support within sight. But my efforts are interrupted by soft clicking and a louder thud.

"Oh good, you're up. Morning!" I hear behind me.

Upon turning, I come face to face with the most beautiful and yet shocking sight ever. Cath's cheeks are pink from the cold outside and her hair is loosely hanging down, framing her pretty face. She smiles at me and lifts up the bag in her hand.

"Sorry, I just went and bought some bread. Didn't want to disturb you. I thought you might like to sleep a bit longer..."

I'm dumbfounded and just stare at her. This can't be—perhaps I'm still asleep and only dreamt about waking.

"Do you remember anything?"

I shake my head—slowly—trying not to upset my sense of balance too much.

"You came by last night, after having a bit too much to drink. I guess you found my note?"

Flashes of last night are coming back to me slowly at last.

God, how embarrassing.

Yes, her note from my bag. That's how I found her house. And by the time I got here, I was pretty angry. I vaguely recall yelling at her about it. Sitting back down again, I start to rub my temples with my fingertips to get my splitting headache under control.

"Oh fuck. I actually said all those things? I'm so sorry," I whisper.

Despite sitting still and focusing as much as I can, I struggle to dig for more memories. My thoughts are interrupted when I feel her hand burning into my shoulder. I hold my breath in an effort to disguise the fact that even a simple touch of hers forces my heartbeat into overdrive.

"Don't worry about it. Hey, I'll be right back," she says.

I'm so deeply lost in thought that I only barely hear the door opening and closing behind me, followed by the sound of running water.

After I accused her of messing me about, what did she say? She had tears in her eyes; I definitely remember that.

Shit, I made her cry. *I'm such an idiot!* And then... she came closer and held me, and... I wish I could be certain whether I'm remembering last night or a dream.

"No, it can't be..."

"What can't be?" she says. I hadn't even noticed her coming back in. She sits down next to me again, legs folded and facing me. The thin fabric of her T-shirt clings around her just enough to show off her perfect, bra-less body. I force myself to look at her face instead.

I wonder why she bothers to put on make-up for work; she's perfect without it.

"Did we...?" I start, not daring to finish the question.

She gives me a wicked smile. "What are you hoping that we did?"

Blood rushes into my cheeks and I just stare at her. Speechless.

"Okay, I'm being unfair." She lets out a giggle, "We kissed. That's it. I wouldn't want to be accused of taking advantage of you while you're out of it."

Her face turns serious. "But I need you to be honest. If what you said last night was just the booze talking… We can just forget about the whole thing."

I'm just shocked. She kissed me. All these images in my head—they're real, no dream. I can barely catch my breath.

What does it all mean? Maybe she was just trying to get me to calm down. After all, I might have scared her coming at her all riled up like that.

"Look, I was being truthful last night," she continues. "I like you. But I thought you weren't interested and I didn't want to seem desperate. I wanted a real chance."

I have so many questions, I don't know where to begin. "Why—"

"I don't want to be your rebound girl. That sort of thing never works out. I'm only interested if you like me for *me*." She looks gorgeous even with that worried frown on her face, or perhaps even more so because of it.

Her words make no sense—she's worried *I'm* not really into *her*? That she'd be a stand-in for Julie? That's laughable.

As much as I know I need to say *something*, the words continue to evade me. The concern on her face is intensifying. I can't stay quiet much longer. *She* has never been the problem; I am.

I hold my breath again and force my hand forward, running my fingertips gently down her cheek. Why doesn't she stop me? I keep expecting her to.

But she doesn't stir, even when I tentatively place my other hand on her shoulder. The moment I coax her towards me ever so slightly, she falls into my arms as though that's where she's wanted to be all along.

How did I do this? She's the kindest person I've ever met, way out of my league in every way. And now she's in my arms, hiding her face in my chest.

All I've ever done was be grumpy and horrible to her. I yelled at her last night, for what? For being nice to me, for *flirting*? What a moron I am.

"I'm so sorry," I say finally. "I've been such a moody bastard all along. You didn't deserve any of it."

I hold her tighter, and nuzzle my face into her soft hair. Her scent is intoxicating. She feels so small in my embrace, so fragile. She has let her defenses down in front of me and it's obvious that this isn't just an act. It's only the two of us here. No audience.

"Sure, I've been upset over Julie, but things changed the moment you walked into the office on your first day. I could hardly stand it sitting next to you every day. I thought if I ignored you, it wouldn't hurt so much that I couldn't have you."

She pulls back and looks up at me, her eyelashes sticky with the remnants of tears as she blinks a few times.

"Well, you have me now," she says.

A smile appears on her lips. She looks like an angel when she smiles.

"Are you hungry?" And she's perceptive as well.

"I guess, but you don't need to make a fuss..." I get up and start looking for the bathroom.

Luckily there aren't many doors to choose from. The first one I try happens to be the correct one. I take one look at myself in the mirror and the same feeling of shock from before hits me again. I look and smell revolting; like I've been bathing in alcohol. *Ugh.*

And I've just had my dream girl pressed into my chest, without her showing the slightest hint of disgust. She seemed to rather enjoy that moment.

The cold tap water feels refreshing against my face, and does wake me some. I still can't accept what's happened.

There's a knock on the door.

"Fresh towels are in the cupboard if you need them... and you're welcome to use the bathrobe hanging on the door," she says.

Okay, so she did notice the smell. *Awkward.*

VIII.

I stretch a few times on the way to the kitchen, feeling quite pleased with myself indeed. He's just there, in the bathroom. I can hear the water running.

He likes me! He has done from the start. This is going much better than I had hoped for.

I know I told him I didn't want to be with him while he's on the rebound. But I was lying, mainly to myself. I would've happily taken any chance of being with him at all.

I've always been a slave to my emotions, but somehow even more so in this instance. How very desperate of me.

Maybe because it's been a while since I've been with someone? No, that can't be it. There is just something special about John. This isn't just a little crush. Though it makes no sense and it's much too soon, I already started to fall for him.

I wonder what he likes for breakfast? I've never seen him eat much at work. Bacon and eggs seem like a safe bet.

Quickly I clear the dirty dishes off the small breakfast bar—the only thing even resembling a dining table which could fit into this place. I hope he hasn't noticed the mess. At least I remembered to tidy the bathroom when I went in just before him.

While the bacon is sizzling away, I quickly run into

the bedroom. What I'm looking for is in these drawers that haven't been opened in ages. Greg's old stuff has to still be in here somewhere—all the things he didn't bother taking with him when he left.

Will it make John uncomfortable to wear my ex's old clothes? Then again, it's all I have to offer. I finally locate some sweats and a T-shirt. They should fit, hopefully. After all, Greg was quite a big guy as well, but that is where his resemblance to John ends.

I carry them back into the kitchen with me and leave them on a bar stool.

"Wow, that smells great," John says when he reappears a few minutes later.

He looks so tempting in the fleecy dark blue robe from the bathroom. Thoughts of what's hiding underneath distract me immensely as I plate up the food.

"Oh, it's nothing fancy," I say as I turn back to face the counter again. "Tea or coffee?"

"Tea please," John says.

"I found some clothes—see if they fit. I figured you might want to wear something fresh." I say while busying myself with the tea for longer than necessary.

But the more I look in his direction, the more obviously my body starts to react. My nipples are already poking against my T-shirt and a familiar warm sensation is building up in my lower abdomen.

It took a lot of effort for me to be decent last night. I felt his warm urgent breaths against my lips and his tongue feverishly seeking out mine.

He wanted me. It was so obvious.

But I owed it to myself to take things slow. I refused to give myself up without knowing for sure that he wants *me for me*. Not this time. I've learned my lesson.

And even if I had been sure of his intentions then, I would have wanted him to be lucid enough to remember every second of it.

As soon as I put the tea on the bar, where the food is already waiting, John comes back in wearing the clothes I found. If anything, they're ever so slightly loose on him. He looks delicious even so.

I can't take my eyes off him. Before I know it, I'm checking him out from head to toe. Hopefully he doesn't think I'm a total nympho.

We sit down at opposite ends of the bar. His body language is stiff and reserved again.

"So, whose are these then? They seem a bit, umm, big for you," he asks.

"An ex left them behind," I say, before taking a big bite of toast. "But don't worry, he's not about to come back looking for them."

"Ah. Right."

We eat quietly, every so often sneaking a look at each other. The food seems to be doing him good; he is starting to look better with every bite. The colour is returning to his face. But he's also quieter than before. More thoughtful. Something seems to be bothering him.

"More?" I ask, as soon as he's emptied his plate.

"No, that's okay. Thanks." His eyes wander around the kitchen, back over the empty plates and finally focus on me.

"I guess I should head home, then," he says. His tone suggests it's more of a question than an observation.

"If you want..." *Please don't go!* "Do you have any plans this weekend?"

"Not really," he answers.

God, this is awkward. I really don't want him to leave yet. Not now that we're finally starting to work out where we stand.

"Well, you're more than welcome to stay if you like. I haven't got anything on either. I was just going to chill and watch some movies. Or whatever you'd like to do..."

I don't even dare to breathe until I get an answer.

"Sure," he says.

Is it just me, or does he sound equally relieved?

His expression has relaxed again and his eyes meet mine. We just stare. Time seems to slow.

I wonder if he can feel the same flutter in his chest that I feel. The same ticklish sensation in his stomach. The same magnetism between us. How my hands are drawn towards him at any given moment.

Of course, that's why I've been extra touchy-feely at work.

I don't do the casual gestures or little touches that come so naturally to a lot of people. Normally, I'm extremely reserved, distant even.

The one time I remember hugging Jason even was at his dad's funeral. And he's like my best friend and big brother rolled into one.

But lately, I've been fighting a constant urge to throw myself at John. Why am I still fighting? He seemed willing enough, earlier!

I slip off the bar stool, taking a step in his direction. His eyes have widened, and breaths sped up again. He swallows hard. What a sweetheart—so nervous, just like me.

But we can't both be shy, I tell myself. Or nothing will ever happen.

"I've been wanting to do this again so badly," I breathe, my lips almost touching his, but I hold back. I need his reassurance.

"Me too," he whispers back at me.

He smells of my shower gel and clean laundry. And still there's this unmistakable scent holding it all together—*his* scent. I can't hold back any longer. I guide his hands onto my waist. Then, I slide my own hands up over his arms, shoulders and around his neck and pull myself close to him.

His lips are as soft as I remember from last night. Just perfect. Our initial contact hits me like an electric shock. The tension that had built up throughout the morning is somewhat released. We're free now.

As we kiss deeply and passionately, his strong arms tighten around me once more. He gets off his stool as well, bending down to allow me better reach. He may have started off shy, but his kisses are determined.

I can feel his need for me in his movements. His hands explore the contours of my back, fingertips gently massage my shoulder blades through my thin cotton T-shirt. I slip my hands around his waist as well, tugging at him to hold me tighter. He grabs me around the small of my waist, twirls me around and lifts me up onto his bar stool.

At last my face is exactly at his level. I put my arms around his neck again, running my fingers through his damp hair. My legs spread to allow his body closer to mine.

"You're amazing," I tell him.

One of my hands slips down the back of his T-shirt caressing his smooth, soft skin on his shoulders, while the other remains in his hair, playing and tugging softly.

"Liar," he responds.

I pull back and look into his deep amber eyes again. So innocent and naked. His defences are down for me now. I cover his cheek in kisses, before travelling down his neck. His head and shoulders twitch, trapping me, but I keep on licking and sucking on his silky skin, just underneath his ear and where his neck reaches his shoulder.

A groan escapes his lips and his hands freeze on my back. He's rigid in my arms, clinging to me tightly.

"Stop—I can't," he says, gasping for air.

I release my hold on him and look him in the eyes.

"What's wrong?" I ask.

"I can't hold back," he says, trying his best to avoid eye contact. Looks like the walls are back up.

"You don't need to hold back." I run my hand through his hair again.

"I can't do this, not yet," he whispers.

His statement confuses me; I hadn't foreseen anything like this.

"You don't have to. There's no rush," I say softly, trying to hide my concern. I smile at him and give him a soft peck on his lips. "You choose, whatever you want to do and when. We can take things slowly."

Finally, he looks back into my eyes. His relief is obvious.

But now I'm worried. Where did I go wrong? Maybe he is still too sore about his ex after all?

"Thanks. I'm sorry about this..." His hand reaches up to caress my cheek with the back of his fingers. "I need you to know, it's not you. I'm just... I want things to be perfect. This is huge for me."

I swallow and blink a few times, while studying his face. He seems genuine. I do hope he doesn't think I'm easy for wanting to rush into things with him.

"Right. Well, how about those movies then...?" I try to change the topic while slipping off the bar stool. He holds me back by my arm just as I try to head toward the sofa.

"I mean it. It's not you. I just never thought I'd end up here. I'm still sort of expecting that I'll wake up alone in my own bed with a massive hangover and this will all have been a dream," he says. "I don't want to mess this up. I don't want you to do anything that you'll regret."

Regret, me? I shake my head in disbelief.

"Why would you mess anything up?" I wonder aloud.

His face falls and his voice is a whisper. "I hardly know what I'm doing."

Oh, damn. He's still nervous! That's something I can relate to. I'm not naturally confident either. There were times not too long ago when just making a simple phone call would give me a mild panic attack.

"Well, you could've fooled me." I smile at him.

I hand him the remote while we sit down on the sofa.

"You pick, I've not seen any of them yet."

I purposely sit extra close to him, even though the sofa is spacious enough. He presses play and the movie starts, but I'm not even sure which one it is; neither do I care. His warmth right next to me, the memory of our kiss, it all adds up to make me painfully aware of even the slightest movement or sound. His breathing is calmer than before, but he's still tense, sitting straight up with his hands on his thighs.

With both legs folded underneath me, I wiggle back into the plush sofa, brushing against his leg. His arm twitches and he holds his breath. Then he raises his arm and puts it around me. I don't hesitate to move closer against him and rest my head on his shoulder. I can feel him sigh. Why does he continue to be so nervous? If I'm willing, and he is too, then what's causing all this anxiety?

I turn towards him and upon finding his other arm, I slip my hand underneath to hold him tight. That was all the encouragement he needed. I'm engulfed in his embrace, pressing myself tightly against his chest. His heartbeat is rapid, in tune with the eerie background music of the movie we're not really watching.

I can feel his breath against my hair. It tickles slightly, putting me even more on edge. I can be patient for him, I tell myself. With my eyes closed I focus on my own breathing now, forcing it to slow down already.

It's not really working...

"Why?" His voice interrupts my attempts at calming myself.

"Why, what?" I ask.

"This. You, me..." He hesitates.

"I don't understand. Why not?" I respond.

"I just never had anyone interested in me like that before," he says, his voice sounding even flatter than before.

"But I thought— What about your ex?" I still ask the question, even though I clearly remember what Amanda told me. I'm not about to humiliate him by telling him I already know too much, though.

He swallows hard and shakes his head. "She never kissed me once like you have. I should've seen it, but I guess I didn't have anything to compare it to. The whole time we were together was a lie. When she left, I thought that's it. My one chance, gone."

"That's why you've been so upset, even before you found out about *them*," I say, holding him tighter.

"Initially. Until you came along and then I couldn't stop wondering, what if..." His voice is almost a whisper now. His gentle kisses burn through my hair, on top of my head and neck.

"She sounds crazy," I say.

When I look up, I'm overwhelmed by the sadness I see in his eyes.

"How dare she?"

I hold his face in my hands again and kiss him on the lips. My whole being aches for him. I desperately want to show him that things can and will be different from now on.

"And before her?" I ask.

"Nothing. Girls weren't interested. Dan was always the popular one in my family. If any girl spoke to me throughout secondary school, it was to be introduced to him. Same thing at college..."

The way he says his name suggests he doesn't think much of his brother at all. They clearly had issues long before that *Julie* woman even turned up.

"Oh well. School was pretty similar for me. I was never popular either—" Jason, on the other hand…

He cuts me off with further kisses. But I'm not done with my questions.

"Last night, you said it was like being fifteen all over again. What did you mean?" I ask.

"Oh, that." He averts his eyes from mine. "There was a girl in my class, she'd only just joined the school that term. She seemed nice. Different. One of the other girls in our class told me she wanted to be my date for the upcoming school dance but was too shy to ask for herself. In the end it was just a set-up, a joke. They were all in on it."

"Oh shit, I'm so sorry," I whisper, pressing my cheek

against his and putting my arms around his neck. For one person to experience so many let-downs… It's obvious what his anxiety stems from now.

"Never mind, that was a long time ago. But…" He takes a deep breath. "I still don't understand how *this* happened. Why do you like me?"

"What's there not to like? You're kind, caring, honest, you have a great sense of humor, you're really smart—" I start.

"Yeah, sure. All good reasons to be just friends and nothing more," he interrupts me.

"You're strong, and don't seem to care what people think, loyal, I feel like I could trust you with anything…" I continue.

He shakes his head. "Hold on. Take a good look at me and back at yourself. Why would *you* want to be with a guy *like me*? You could have anyone. Richard has been—"

"Don't you mention his name in this context! He's uber-creepy! Never in a million years would I ever consider—" I shudder instead of finishing that sentence. Just thinking about him makes my skin crawl.

John just looks at me with an amused glint in his eyes and a smile playing on his lips.

"Ha, you really hate him, don't you!"

"Is it *that* obvious?" I ask, grinning back at him.

"My point still stands though—why would you ever like a guy like me?" he asks again.

"I thought I had just made it clear that you do appear to be quite a catch." I innocently bat my eyelashes.

"You know what I mean... look at you, you're absolutely stunning and I'm..." He gestures down at himself, and it's even more obvious where this is going.

This is one conversation that comes up every time. I just hope he'll be able to accept my answer. Unlike Greg.

"You're a big guy, so what? I don't mind," I respond.

Sweetheart, you have no idea how much I don't mind. It's the first thing I noticed about him.

"You're odd." He sighs and pulls me back into his arms. "But I'm glad for it."

The film is still on, preparing for its climactic finish in which the main character stabs the baddie with a huge kitchen knife, before making her escape.

"Which movie was this, anyway?" I ask as the credits roll.

He just laughs in response. At last, he sounds genuinely at ease.

I cuddle up even closer. God knows just being this close to John has me all hot and bothered. But at the same time, it's a revelation how amazing it is to just sit here, enjoying each other's company and innocent affection. Where did all these feelings come from in such a short time? I've never fallen so quickly for anyone.

"Oh, shit. That Christmas bash, that's tonight, isn't it?" I remember.

"Right. Fairly stupid timing if you ask me. Were you thinking of going?" he asks.

"Well, I thought, with me being the new girl and all.

Maybe I should show my face for a bit."

"I guess, yeah," he says.

"You weren't planning to?" I ask.

He shrugs.

"Well, we could go together. I mean, if you feel like it," I suggest.

"What, officially? Like, you want to literally go *together*?" He sounds surprised.

It occurs to me that I don't really care about how we'll be perceived. As long as he's fine with it.

"Unless it makes you uncomfortable. I'd ask if there was a policy against that sort of thing, but I've been hearing plenty of chatter to suggest there isn't. Or at least there isn't when your name is *Richard*," I say.

"Me? Uncomfortable? Hell no. But you do realize that people will talk?" he says.

"Where would Sharon and her gang be without fresh gossip?" I smile at him.

"Richard will be annoyed," he remarks.

"That's his problem then. Plus he might back off when he realizes I'm taken."

We sit quietly for another minute or so.

"You're serious, aren't you?" John asks.

"About?"

"You really don't care what anyone will say?" He still sounds uncertain.

"I don't even like any of them. Out of everyone at work, I've only ever cared about what *you* think of me. So, as long as it wouldn't cause you any trouble..." I say.

"No, no trouble. This is just unexpected, that's all."

He shakes his head a few times. "I still don't know what I ever did to get you to like me."

"I have an idea what you can do now to get me to like you even better," I say with a naughty smile. I move back and lie against the armrest of the empty half of the sofa, motioning him to come closer. He does until he is right on all fours, on top of me.

"Kiss me again," I whisper. His eyes darken as he rests on his elbows either side of me. I kiss him hungrily, our bodies pressed together and his lips on mine. I'm sandwiched between the sofa and his soft bulk, so excited I can barely breathe.

He stops and starts to lift himself off me.

"I'm sorry, I'm crushing you..."

But I don't let him go and pull him down again.

"You're not," I gasp. "Carry on."

It doesn't take much to convince him. Our mouths merge, tongues entwined, in the most mind-blowing kiss I have ever experienced. For someone who's supposedly not had a lot of practice with the opposite sex, he sure knows what he's doing.

My fingertips run up his arms simultaneously, teasing his bare skin under the sleeves of his T-shirt, up to his shoulders and over his shoulder blades. He feels so smooth and flawless, I wish I could have a taste.

I can feel him shudder under my every touch, involuntarily grinding up against me. His arousal is blatantly obvious, pressing rock hard into my thigh. I was already breathless and now he has reached a similar state. His lips find my neck, impatiently kissing and sucking in between ragged breaths. I writhe underneath him, rubbing my thigh against his hard cock in encouragement.

There is so much more I could do, if only I could reach.

He moans into my ear. What a deep, sexy voice he has.

"Ohh, I can't—" He stops mid-sentence, while I just hang on to him, feeling every single muscle in his back tense up together underneath my fingertips. I lift myself up against him as far as I can manage. He starts to twitch and shudder, and I just hold on, biting softly into his neck, enjoying the last primal groan that escapes his lips before he sinks into me, slowly relaxing all over, pinning me into the sofa cushion under his full weight.

"Shit, I'm so sorry," he finally manages after catching his breath.

"Shh," I say. "That was so hot! Best kiss ever." My hands are still in his T-shirt, caressing his back before circling over his shoulders.

He has moved down a little bit, with his face resting against my shoulder. I remove my hand from his shirt and wrap my arm around him as far as I can reach. He nuzzles his face underneath, and lets out a deep sigh.

"This is what I was worried about. That I'd lose it." He doesn't sound too worried, though. Just content.

I lift up my head and plant a kiss on his hair. Maybe this release was exactly what he needed to calm down already.

"It's good to let go sometimes. And for a second

there, I was worried you didn't want me as much as I want you," I whisper.

He remains silent, taking slower and deeper breaths. Finally, he lifts up one arm and takes my hand, kissing my knuckles and putting it over the side of his head, covering his eyes.

"You are a bit odd indeed." He sighs again.

I can't help but smile. "Odd or not. You're stuck with me now."

PART II.

I.

The room is quiet when I wake up. The TV is on standby and it looks like it's already dark outside. John is still partially on top of me, breathing deeply and regularly. I stretch my legs as much as I can without disturbing him.

Wonder what time it is?

John wakes the moment I try to adjust my arms. He lifts himself up until we're facing each other.

"Seems I fell asleep on you..." He clears his throat.

"Or, I fell asleep underneath you. Not sure who started it." I grin at him.

I glance at the clock on the DVD player. 6:30 pm. We'd better get moving.

"We're still going to the party, right?" I ask.

"Yeah, I guess."

"I think you need a change of clothes. This is perhaps a bit too casual." Still grinning, I point down at the dark patch that has spread from the crotch of his sweat pants onto my thigh.

"Oh, damn. My place isn't far from here... I can quickly go change while you get yourself ready?" he suggests.

"Or, you give me five minutes now and we can stop at yours on the way to the venue," I say.

He gets up and I rush into the bedroom. Luckily, I had already decided what to wear ages ago; little black satin dress, black lace stilettos. I make a poor attempt at disguising the smell of sex that's undoubtedly still hanging around me with some perfume.

John is in the bathroom, with the tap running. By the time I'm done brushing my hair and slapping on a bit of lipstick and mascara he comes out in last night's clothes.

"Ready?" I ask, while putting in the second one of the pair of dangly silver earrings I found on the bedside table.

He turns to look at me and inhales sharply through his teeth. His eyes are drawn straight to the plunging neckline of my dress, down over the silky black fabric that clings around my curves in just the right places before ending midway up my thigh.

"You look..." he says finally. "Wow."

"Glad you like it." I smile at him.

We rush out the door while I'm still in the process of putting on my coat.

I put my arm through his as we walk briskly down the street, battling the evening chill. But sure enough, we reach his flat within five minutes. We make our way up the stairwell to the first floor.

Before unlocking his front door, he pauses and turns to me. "I'm not exactly prepared for company..."

"Don't worry about it."

He leads me in through the hallway and into the living room.

The flat is in utter chaos. Empty take-out containers, bottles on the floor. It's obvious that housework has been the last thing on his mind lately. I try not to stare and clear some space on the sofa before taking a seat.

"I'll wait here, you get changed," I tell him.

His eyes are furiously darting around the room, the embarrassment written on his face.

"Really, it's fine. My place looks like this too sometimes," I lie.

Finally, he disappears into the other room, leaving me alone with my thoughts.

Considering the state of this room, it's obvious how much he's been suffering this past month. As shocking as some of his behaviour in the office was, that was just the tip of the iceberg.

To think that I was worrying about the few dirty dishes in my kitchen this morning. What a waste of energy.

Things can only get better from here, surely?

If only I can get him to come out of his shell a little. He's still so tense around me. How on earth can I make him feel more at ease? Perhaps it's time to grow up and not let my own insecurities get in the way anymore. It should be safe to assume he's as interested in me as I am in him. I might have to take the lead with him and show him just how far I'm willing to take things.

Ignoring the mess for a moment, I continue to scrutinise the room. The cabinet opposite the sofa is as one would expect: a TV, stereo, some CDs. On the opposite wall hangs a painting.

I get up to take a closer look. It's haunting—an empty forest, foggy and mysterious. The scene draws me in closer. The painting itself is unframed, just oil on canvas, his name signed in the corner.

"Beautiful," I whisper, feeling the texture of the paint underneath my fingertips. Clearly there is a lot more to him than what I've been seeing at the office. A creativity I could not have guessed at.

"Oh, that old thing." I hear behind me.

His breath caresses the side of my neck and I feel my skin contract in waves of tingly goose bumps. My breaths stall as his arms wrap around my waist and his lips touch my naked shoulder. I turn to face him, still breathless.

"Love the suit!" I say while running my fingers up the collar of his jacket and down again across the tie.

Every day at work he's been in trousers and shirts, which were nice in their own way. But this is something else entirely.

"Very sexy." I smile.

He takes a step back. "Whatever you say."

I pull him back gently by his tie, and chastely kiss his lips before wiping the lipstick marks off. "Let's go?"

By the time we come out, it has started to drizzle. We're lucky to find a cab right outside his building.

He doesn't say much the whole way, but from the corner of my eye I can see he keeps looking in my direction. So does the driver for that matter. Back and forth from me to him, through the rear-view mirror, as if he can sense the sexual tension between us.

I pretend not to notice and just sit still, holding his hand. I'm hatching a little plan to surprise him. Hopefully my scheme will coax him more out of his shell.

I'll have to do some reconnaissance too once we get to the hotel.

Meanwhile he's starting to fidget, growing more nervous the closer we get.

It doesn't matter to me what our colleagues will think.

I'm hoping to get Dick off my back once and for all. And the girls have been asking me for weeks whether I'm bringing a date to the party. I never had an answer before, but it's going to be pretty obvious now.

I'm just so glad how this has turned out so far. Only twenty-four hours ago I hardly dared to dream that he had feelings for me too. And look at us now. The thought makes me smile.

"What's funny?" John asks.

"I'm just happy you're here with me," I respond while squeezing his hand tighter.

The cabbie's stares have become even more intrusive. Normally that wouldn't bother me, if only he paid more attention to the road.

Finally, we arrive; in one piece.

The hotel the company has booked looks quite fancy. That's probably why Amanda wouldn't shut up about it for weeks. There is a sign at reception pointing towards a large conference room: 'Aspect Christmas Ball'. I roll my eyes. *Christmas.* It's barely December.

Some familiar faces arrive along with us, but nobody I know by name. We leave our coats and follow the signs inside.

While approaching the conference room, I catch a glimpse of a dark hallway that leads from the main hotel lobby. I'll have to check it out later.

John still looks uneasy. I put my arm through his and scan the room. Sparkly lights hanging from the ceiling, countless round tables laid out with shiny white china and centerpieces of holly dotted with silver and black Christmas baubles. It's almost blinding, like a glitter bomb has gone off in the middle of the room.

There's a podium at the far end of the hall. I cringe at the prospect of listening to managerial speeches over dinner. Why do they even bother? With a bit of luck, I'll be buzzed enough not to care by that time.

"Let's get a drink," I suggest, pointing towards the bar in the corner.

"Cath!" I hear a familiar high-pitched voice towards

my right.

Amanda walks over to me in long strides. "I wasn't sure you'd come."

She stops in her tracks when she spots my hand on his arm. "Oh. Hey, John."

"Amanda," he responds.

Awkward silence.

I turn to Amanda, and greet her confused expression with a radiant smile. "Hi! Yes, of course I came. Even managed to get myself a date."

"Yeah, um. I didn't realise you guys were this close," she says.

Yeah, neither did I, until this morning.

"We were just heading to the bar, you coming?" I ask.

"No, that's okay..." She raises the nearly full glass in her hand to make her point.

We leave her standing by herself.

"It'll be about five minutes before everyone knows," John remarks dryly.

"Good. I'll have a white wine in the meantime."

I watch him walk to the bar; he does wear that suit extremely well. I may have watched one too many James Bond movies growing up, which inspired this fascination with formal wear. But there is one crucial difference, unlike Bond, John has no idea how hot he is. And that makes him all the more irresistible.

Sooner or later I'll have to be completely honest with him, but I don't want to scare him off. I remember all too well how things turned out with Greg when I opened up to him.

John is talking to the bartender, and I can't keep my eyes off him. Everything else around me blurs into the background. John turns around, both drinks in hand, and walks towards me. It's a sight to behold for multiple reasons.

The obvious sparkle in his eyes is something I've never seen before. For weeks there's been this intense sadness around him. Tonight, he's transformed. A spring in his step, renewed confidence in his movements. And that smile.

This beats even my very first memory of him, when he caught my eye during the job interview. What's even better is now he's mine.

Finally, he's standing right in front of me, offering me my glass. My eyes are glued to his. There's so much to uncover. In the amber depths I see tenderness, warmth, perhaps even love? Could it be, or is it just wishful thinking?

When I accept my glass, our fingers brush against each other ever so briefly. My heart jumps. I hope I never get used to this feeling.

"Cheers," I say.

I take a sip of wine to calm myself, but still can't bear to look away.

"I see you already have a drink. Too bad, I was going to offer you one."

Turning sharply, I see Dick standing a few paces beside us. He looks even more unpleasant than normally. Perhaps the gossip has reached him already.

"John." He nods, with a dark expression on his face.

"Richard," John responds.

I glance back and forth between the both of them as they stare each other down. I do hope there won't be a scene.

I clear my throat. "Maybe we should find our seats before dinner starts?"

Dick just gives me a disapproving look and walks off, probably in search of a more willing victim.

"Okay, that went well," I comment.

John shakes his head. "I wonder what his fucking problem is."

"Guess he doesn't enjoy rejection. The creep," I say, shuddering at the memory of Dick cornering me by the drinks machine last week.

John puts his arm around me, and whispers a promise in my ear. "Don't worry. He tries anything and I'll kick his scrawny arse."

Love this protective streak in him. I slide my arm underneath his jacket and around his lower back. I pause when my hand reaches his side. Just like that, I'm turned on again. But my explorations will have to wait.

That's the awkward part of the evening done with; I hope.

III.

We meander around some of the tables. Each is marked by department name, but there are no individual name cards.

It's starting to get quite busy now as more of our colleagues have arrived. The mood is generally good, but then again, I'm living a dream today, so I might be biased. Also, I'm all the more pleased now that Dick is nowhere in sight.

The wall clock strikes quarter to eight. I'm guessing nothing will happen for at least fifteen minutes.

I let go of John and excuse myself. "Ladies' room, I'll be right back."

"Sure. I'll keep a chair for you if necessary." He points at the table marked with our department name; 'Purchasing—Semiconductors'.

"Cool."

I head for the door and find the restrooms just opposite. But I'm not really looking for those.

Instead, I want to explore the dark hallway I'd spotted on our way in. Nobody is around as far as I can tell.

There are two doors a good twenty feet away. I carefully open the furthest one labelled 'Staff only'. A table with folded stacks of clean laundry greets me inside. I check the backside of the door and spot a key in the lock. As if the hotel staff knew to plan for all eventualities. This will be absolutely perfect.

I peep out to check that the coast is clear, and head straight back to the party.

As soon as I find John, one of the hotel staff steps up to the microphone.

"Ladies and gentlemen. Please be informed that dinner will start at eight-thirty. In the meanwhile, you may help yourselves to champagne."

And indeed, waiters appear with trays of glasses of bubbly. It's unlikely to be the good stuff, but I'm not fussed.

I pick up two glasses from the first tray that passes by, and hand one to John. "Cheers!"

"If I didn't know any better, I'd wonder if you were trying to get me drunk," he says.

"Yeah, you're just *so* charming when you've had a few," I tease.

We take a few sips. The cold, fizzy champagne goes straight to my head. I'm emboldened enough to put my plan into action.

I glance at the clock once more and set down my almost empty glass.

"I'm going out into the hallway, you keep an eye on your phone, when I text you, come out too and head to the right," I whisper in his ear.

He frowns for a moment, but then nods in agreement.

On my way to the exit, I can feel him watching as I walk away. I try to make it sexy; hips swaying from side to side just enough to attract his full attention. With the heels and slightly clingy dress, it should be a good show.

Hopefully the view is putting him in exactly the right mood for what is to come.

The hallway is still empty and dark, thank God. I get my phone out and send him a quick message.

'Now!'

He must have been quite keen, because he doesn't make me wait. *Good.*

I give him a quick wave from the doorway of the laundry room. He joins me inside and I immediately turn to lock the door.

The room is dim; lit only by one of those always-on safety lights on the far end wall. I hang up my clutch bag on a hook on the wall and turn back to face him.

"I simply had to get you alone for a bit." I run his silk tie through my fingers. "Because with so many people around, I haven't been able to appreciate you all dressed up like this."

I pull him against me, and kiss him deeply on his lips. He immediately responds, with both hands on my back pulling me in tighter. I let out a moan while he explores my neck with further kisses.

Don't know if it was the wine or a permanent increase in confidence, but he's certainly got the message. One of his hands slides down onto the small of my back before cupping my ass.

I moan louder, spurring him on and he starts squeezing my bum. Gently at first, but soon his movements get firmer.

It feels so good. I press myself up against him. My thigh rubs against his, my hard nipples brush his chest as his belly presses against mine. He angles his face upwards and finds my lips with his again.

"Oh God, you turn me on so much," I whisper.

Both my hands now make their way to his jacket collar, and pushing it off his shoulders.

My chest heaves with heavy fast breaths. I catch him helplessly staring at the view from above. I discard his jacket onto the pile of sheets behind us. One of my hands finds its way to his shirt buttons, slipping two fingers in just above where it's tucked into his trousers, teasing it out and unbuttoning him from the bottom up.

I slip my hand under his shirt, over his sides, skimming the soft fabric of his undershirt until I reach his bare shoulders. It makes me dizzy to be this close to him, but I can't stop.

He's completely still, his forehead against mine and eyes closed, breathing in short bursts against my lips. One hand still rests on my arse, the other on my side just above the hip. His growing erection is pressed hard into my lower abdomen. The exact same spot is clenched together with arousal and I can feel my panties getting soaked.

"Wait. I've never done this..." he whispers.

I softly bite and tug at his bottom lip before responding.

"It's my first semi-public hook-up too."

"No. I mean I've *never* done *this*. Ever." His eyes are wide, not just with nerves but perhaps fear?

He just looks at me with his lips pressed together tightly, as if he's desperate to hear my reaction.

Finally, it hits me. I don't know how I could have misread his earlier hints? I'd made so many assumptions that I didn't read the signs. Despite the unfortunate experience with his ex, John is still a virgin! That's why he wanted to take it slow. His remarks earlier about not knowing what he's doing. It all makes sense now.

I slip both my hands over the gorgeously smooth skin on his shoulders and press my lips against him for another kiss. The tension in his eyes softens until he closes them, losing himself again.

I don't mind. The thought that I might end up being his first does nothing to discourage me. Instead, it turns me on further. I was right to take the lead tonight. That's okay, I'm ready for him whenever he is.

"Just enjoy it, then. Let me take care of you."

I release one hand from his neck and run it down his chest and belly over the bulge in his trousers. He gasps and presses his face into my neck. My fingers working furiously now to release his belt and undo his trousers, my other hand takes his from my side and slides it forward onto my breast. He gently squeezes it, driving me even more insane.

My other hand successfully opens his fly, slips inside and into his boxers. His cock feels warm, solid. I tease it out and reach for his balls. He groans and shudders against me, causing every inch of my body to respond to his pleasure. Grabbing his cock once more, I start to rub my hand up and down his full length.

"I just want to make you feel good... Do you still want me to slow down?" I ask, fully aware of how hard it would be to backtrack now.

For either of us.

"God, no," John moans.

The moment I offer my lips to his, he eagerly kisses me again. As though he can't get enough of me as I can't get enough of him. This seems to be the only way he knows how to express his desires to me, before breathlessness and urgent groans force him to abandon it all.

I tighten my grip on him. How thick and solid he feels in my hand, I get shivers down my spine just imagining how he'd feel inside of me. I lift my leg up slightly so I can rub my thigh against his balls, and stroke him, slowly at first, then faster, in between circling his foreskin with my thumb. His hips grind at me, setting the pace, which is progressively getting more intense. I try to keep up.

He's oblivious to his surroundings now, his breathing strained like it was earlier today on the sofa. He's close, I can feel it. I reach around with my other hand and grab a towel from the table, pushing it between us. He starts to shiver, his hips spasm violently and I feel his cock squirming and pulsating against my grip. He lets out a last muffled groan into my shoulder as cum starts to squirt out into my hand.

His arms surround me, holding me so tight, I'm completely overwhelmed by him.

"Fuck," he stammers. "Fucking hell."

Rather than speak, I just kiss his neck a few times and enjoy watching him catch his breath.

"Not sure what I did to deserve any of this," he says.

He lets go and looks at me, eyes clouded by the orgasm that has just washed over him. His expression is priceless, and I can't help grinning while wiping the lipstick stains off him.

"Told you, you look fucking sexy in a suit."

I crumple up the soiled towel and throw it in the first bin I come across, then head over to the sink. While I wash my hands, he buttons his shirt back up and zips up his trousers.

As I finish drying my hands with another clean towel, I hear footsteps coming up behind me. His hand runs all the way down my back, causing me to twitch and lean back into his touch.

"Mmm, has anyone ever told you that you look quite spectacular yourself, especially in this dress?"

After catching my breath again, I turn and feign innocence, "That hand job has certainly had the desired effect on you, Prince Charming!"

His turn to grin at me.

"Let's head back before we miss dinner," I remind him.

As I reach for to turn the key, he gets a hold of my arm.

"What about you?" he asks.

"Oh, don't worry. You'll have plenty of opportunity to return the favor once we get home."

I give him a little wink and peep out to see if the

coast is clear.

"Okay, follow me."

We hurry out of the corridor and I head straight back to the party, while he takes a detour to the men's room.

He's right; I really could use some relief too. I'm so desperately horny, all this bottled up excitement must be written on my face for all to see. We ought to leave this party early.

I hope John is already plotting his next move.

V. JOHN

My thoughts are going around in circles while I clean myself up in the men's room. So much has happened today and it feels strangely surreal.

Cath is... well I'm not sure I have the words for it. Gorgeous, sexy, perfect. Completely out of my league.

And yet, she wants me anyway.

Every step of the way, I've embarrassed myself. First at home. I couldn't even kiss her without getting hard. She just keeps egging me on too, until I can't take it anymore. Who the hell comes while making out, honestly!

In the laundry room, I suppose it was her intention to take things further, not just mess around like this. I simply couldn't. If I'd just refused her, she would've felt rejected. Telling her the truth was the only logical thing to do, however cringe-worthy it felt.

This game most men appear to play—pretending to be someone else to impress women—I don't know how to do. I've never felt in charge, least of all in relationships. My life has always been in someone else's hands. Cath's in this case. Literally.

She seems so completely sure of what she wants, even if I can't understand why. All I can hope for is that she appreciates my honesty, because frankly I don't know what else I have to offer.

When I confessed to her that I'd never done it, I

expected her to change her mind and run. I expected disappointment. I had assumed that my implied history with Julie had made me a more worthy partner.

Nobody likes a reject.

So I just stood there, at her mercy. Waiting for a shocked laugh or a dismissive remark that never came.

Instead she kissed me, with the same passion she had shown before. I can't decide if she's just a really good actress, or...

She wants me anyway.

At the sink, I opt for the cold tap to try and calm my nerves. She certainly knew what to do, in that laundry room. My God, it felt so good. Indeed, even if she hadn't touched me, I would've finished anyway. Like a bloody hormonal teenager.

Shaking my head, I take a few more deep breaths to try and rid myself of the lingering feeling of embarrassment.

She seemed to like it.

I'm determined to learn what else she likes. Only then will I be worthy of her.

* Cath *

"So, Cath." Dick's voice startles me.

Where the hell did he come from? He leans in closer, with a dark expression on his face.

"You know, we don't take kindly to employees dating each other. It distracts from work."

"Oh? So it's only acceptable when *you* do it?" I hiss back at him.

If looks could kill... Dick's face turns a darker shade of red.

"We could've had something good, you and I. But to then turn up with John as your date, just to spite me," he complains.

He must have had a few too many glasses of champagne if he thinks this approach is going to work. It's starting to piss me off.

"You honestly think this is about *you*?!"

Fuelled by rage as well as wine, I gather the courage to tell him exactly what's what.

"Look, let me make something very clear for you," I start. "I'm not interested in you that way and never have been. And if you don't leave me be, I promise you I will cause serious trouble. I'll make a complaint."

I squint at him. "I can be very convincing, believe me."

Dick backs away. I'm not sure whether it was my words, or the fact that John is now right behind me, his hand resting protectively on my shoulder.

"What did *he* want?" He sounds tense.

"The usual, but I gave him a piece of my mind. I think he'll give up now."

I reach for his hand on my shoulder as we start walking away. Our table, and four pairs of suspicious eyes, await us.

. Before we even reached the table, Amanda and three more of the gang of clones had already taken seats. Despite their lunchroom interrogations, not one of them brought a date tonight.

By the time we get within earshot, everyone's quiet. It's obvious what—or who—tonight's main topic of discussion is.

It should have been awkward, sitting there under everyone's scrutiny, but silence has never bothered me. Well into the main course of tender, slow cooked venison with a rich red wine reduction, I am quite happy to ignore everyone and everything around me. Except John, of course.

We steal glances at each other constantly. Every so often, I brush my foot against his leg underneath the table as if unintentionally. And every time, I enjoy watching him stir while my heart skips a beat or two as well.

My hunger for food is nearly sated but I am still left wanting after our little encounter earlier. Now my impatience is growing to a point where it's becoming hard to ignore.

The waiters reappear to take away the empty plates. It almost looks like a well-choreographed dance. As soon as they disappear, others arrive with dessert.

Dainty little circles of chocolate cheesecake, but with a hint of Christmas spice.

As amazing as the food is, it fails to distract me from the other type of dessert I crave.

With every bite, the heady aroma of spiced chocolate overwhelms my palate. Yet, I can't help but fantasise about how John might pleasure me when we get home. He has so far shown himself to be much more skilled with his lips than he's giving himself credit for.

His willingness to return the favour earlier was promising. What he lacks in experience, he seems to make up for in attentiveness and enthusiasm.

Just as we finish our dishes, the CEO steps up to say a few words. I don't even bother to listen.

Our table is cleared one final time, and everyone around us starts to get up. Alcohol has been flowing freely all evening. Crowds are heading toward the dance floor, but I have other ideas.

"Do you think we'll be awfully missed if we leave now?" I whisper in John's ear. "I'd prefer to have you all to myself for the rest of the night."

He gives me a crooked smile. We both know where this is going.

"Oh, they'll notice. But, do you care?"

VI.

We get up and make our way to the exit to get our coats back from reception. There's a taxi waiting outside already.

"Your place or mine?" I ask while finally succumbing to temptation and nibbling on John's neck. He gives the cabbie my address and puts his arm around me. I rest my head on his shoulder for the rest of the journey, blissfully still with my eyes only half open, taking in the moment. The scent of his skin has become so familiar already.

I wonder how far he'll go; will I get to take that suit off him tonight? He's growing more and more confident, but I continue to wonder just where his boundaries are now.

This isn't the time and place to ask, though.

We pull up outside my building and he rushes to pay the fare. After getting down first, he makes sure to keep the door open and help me out. That's how proper he is.

I switch places once we get into the building until I'm practically dragging him through the long corridor toward my flat. Once we stumble through the open door, I turn around to give him a quick kiss on the lips.

"Do you still want to take things slow?" I blurt out. *Classy.*

He pauses and takes a long hard look down at me. I

imagine the view down my dress is quite mesmerizing from his angle.

"I..." He takes a deep breath. "You completely overwhelm me. I don't know if I can keep you happy."

"You can, you do!" I respond.

Just having him here with me is more than I was expecting only a day ago!

"Well maybe you were hoping for something different. Someone with more experience, who would know what to do."

"What I'm hoping for is to be with *you*. Get to know *you*. I'm not shy about expressing what I like," I remind him.

"I want to show you how you've been making me feel all day..."

His eyes are still fixed on my cleavage when he starts tracing the neckline of my dress. Then, he follows the contours of my collar bones oh so gently with the tip of his finger.

I shudder and utterly fail at breathing.

"Then follow your instincts and treat me as yours," I say.

I take his hand and pull him along while walking backwards towards the bedroom. Once inside, I kick my shoes off, which sends them flying across the floor

We continue shuffling backwards, until I hit the edge of the bed and crawl on top. I slowly unzip the side of my dress while maintaining eye contact.

His lips are parted slightly and I can hear his breaths speed up again. How I love his excitement. He can't take his eyes off me. Deciding to give him more of a show, I pull up the dress and slip it over my head, revealing the black lace bra and thong I had worn for the occasion.

"Holy shit." He's staring, frozen at the side of the bed.

"Take off your jacket and shoes. Come join me," I say as I lie back against the pillows scattered against the headboard.

He startles into action and does as asked. After struggling a bit with his shoes, he finally crawls onto the bed and lies down on his side. His gaze is fixated on me; on the translucent lacy thong, which barely obscures my shaven pussy from view.

Just as I'd hoped.

When he finally forces his gaze upward, he pauses to appreciate my boobs which are almost spilling out of the matching black push-up bra. I love the attention, how caught up in the moment he is.

I'm aching for him, for his lips, his touch and of course his tongue. My hardened nipples are but a small indicator of the arousal I feel when I'm near him. In reality, the sensation is much more intense than my body is capable of showing.

I reach for his hand, and our fingers caress before threading together.

"Touch me," I beg. "I'm yours."

His hand releases mine and moves across my body, fingertips leaving a trail of goose bumps on my stomach. His fingers might as well be on fire, the way my body remembers his every touch. I sigh and arch up against his hand, spurring him on to explore more. His hand glides over the curve of my waist, then closes firmly on where the thinnest part of my thong sits on my hip.

"Just like that," I moan.

My eyes keep closing involuntarily as I exhale. My arms lie limp beside me, unable and unwilling to interfere. He is free to take things wherever he wants them to go. Everything is so utterly perfect, I dare not rush him.

He sits up and leans over, kissing my other side at the indent of my waist while still digging his fingers into my hip. His breath tickles deliciously, making me even more acutely aware of his every move. I moan louder.

Then he lifts his head, leaves a trail of kisses across my stomach, before reaching my cleavage. He releases my hip and places his hand ever so carefully over the cup of my bra. Excitement rushes over me in waves. I grow breathless. While his fingertips explore the lace pattern, my nipple grows even harder, begging to receive more of his touch.

It amazes me how controlled and focused he is, I would've expected him to go for the whole handful immediately. That's how others have done it before him. But he drags it out and teases me slowly. His fingers run circles over the exposed part of my breast while kissing my chest and neck. Right up to that spot halfway between ear and shoulder, it makes me shudder with delight.

He slips his finger underneath the bra strap and slides it off my shoulder; impatiently I respond by lifting off the bed slightly and unhooking my bra from behind, so it just remains draped across. His expression reminds of a child unwrapping a much-desired Christmas gift.

Bending forward, he plants more soft kisses on my chest, until his mouth reaches the tiny bow in the center of the bra. He lifts the entire thing off me with his teeth and lets it fall onto the bed next to us. His eyes widen as he looks down at my breasts.

Perked up and sore. Pink nipples stand to attention for him.

Leaning down again, he continues to kiss the spot on my chest where he had just left off. He slowly moves down lower and lower. His kisses turn to gentle bites and nibbles. By now I'm panting desperately as the juices inside me start to overflow and soak my thong.

If I hadn't decided to let him set the pace, I would've torn his clothes off already and taken him right then and there.

Patience, I say to myself, *it will be worth it.*

My hand has a mind of its own though and starts to touch the arm he's leaning on. I claw against the fabric of his smooth cotton shirt, but my fingernails slide right over it without any resistance. *What I really want is still obscured!*

He scoops me up underneath my shoulder, lifting me half off the bed, lips meeting in a spectacular fashion. Fused to him in our kiss, I slip my fingers into his hair and greedily arch up toward him to try and feel more of his body against mine.

I hook my leg around his thigh, and grind my hips into him. His hand slips between us, finding my breasts, gently cupping them one after the other, squeezing a little and rolling my nipple between his fingers.

After him making me wait this long, my body reacts intensely. It's as if his fingers shock me, sending pleasure signals throughout my entire being. I let out a few loud moans against his lips, savoring the effects of his seemingly expert touch.

How come he knows just what to do? Better even than I could have asked for.

Our lips release and he lowers me back onto the bed. His face moves down my chest, planting soft teasing kisses all over my skin before reaching one of my boobs. He starts by kissing around the areola and progresses to teasing it with the tip of his tongue, circling around and inwards.

He finally takes my nipple into his mouth, gives it a little suck. Once he starts flicking his tongue against it, I'm done for. I'm consumed by waves of pleasure, building up inside. In between strained breaths I hear myself call out.

"Oh God yes! Don't stop!"

By now, all self-control has evaded me. I dig my nails firmly into his shoulders, which frustratingly are still clothed. He sucks harder and at the same time plays with my other nipple. His fingers and tongue are both gentle yet persistent and in perfect harmony. I tense up, shivering and riding the final wave of pleasure to the most unexpected orgasm I've ever had. If he'd had his shirt off, I'm sure I would've drawn blood.

"Fuuuck!" I cry out, before slumping back into the bed, shuddering while he continues to softly lick first one, then the other nipple.

He sits up to admire his handiwork with a smile.

"Well, this was unexpected," he says. "I thought it would be a lot more difficult."

I'm spent, unable to respond with more than a content moan.

But I'm as surprised as he is.

"I have never— This is new to me too," I breathe.

He lies down next to me, pulling me towards him before wrapping his arms all around me.

"Glad to return the favor," he whispers.

I face him, nuzzle against his neck and explore the creases on his shirt with my fingertips.

"How about we even the playing field and you take this thing off for me," I suggest.

I start to open the top button, when he tenses up and stops me.

When I look at him, I note the subtle crease that has appeared between his eyebrows.

"What's wrong?"

He closes his eyes and shakes his head.

"I don't want you to change your mind," he says after a pause.

I slip my arms around his shoulders and kiss his forehead, cheeks, eyelids and anywhere in between.

"You still worry about that?" I ask.

He shrugs.

"You're in my bed. I've given myself to you, to do with as you please. Yet you think I won't like you with your clothes off?" I kiss him again, this time on the lips.

He remains still, then takes a deep breath before answering.

"I don't know. I'd rather—"

I shake my head and interrupt him. "Look, if I really wanted a skinny guy or a gym nut, none of this would have happened in the first place. I'm not blind."

My lips find his once more. I'm torn, he needs to know I'm serious, but what if I end up freaking him out further?

I breathe in deeply.

"Touch me, here." Taking his hand, I guide it towards my still naked chest and further down over my tummy and side down to my hip. "How does that make you feel?"

His breathing changes immediately, becoming irregular and he opens his eyes, his gaze drawn to my nipples.

"That should be obvious. Extremely turned on," he responds.

It's written on his face, yet his admission still makes me blush.

I run the palm of my hand over his ample stomach upwards until I find his nipples through the fabric. He flinches but doesn't stop me.

"So why should it be any different the other way around?" I breathe. "I love how you feel when I touch you, or when you're pressed up against me. The only way it can possibly get any better is if it's skin on skin."

"But—"

He needs to hear it. Consequences be damned.

"I told you earlier today I didn't mind that you're a bigger guy," I continue. "That was an understatement."

He looks confused.

"I like that about you. Everyone has a type. You're mine." I look into his eyes, almost expecting to see some sign that he doesn't believe me, or worse. That he thinks I'm a freak.

But instead, the opposite happens. He seems to relax a little. Thankfully he doesn't question me, or push the topic any further. Instead, he reaches over to the light switch on the wall.

The room is pitch black while my eyes adjust. John is no longer by my side, yet I can still feel his movements through the mattress.

Shortly after, his hand seeks out mine and pulls me up and off the duvet. We both slide underneath the covers together. I seek out his arms and can feel his warm skin burn against me.

I get closer and instinctively bury my face in his chest. His chest hair tickles my nose, but I refuse to move away. His arms close around me, and I'm enveloped in heaven.

It's glorious.

Not being able to see heightens my other senses, stirring up even more of that same feverish excitement that brought me to orgasm earlier. My hand is drawn to his shoulder first, and his skin feels soft as silk. He shudders a little as I move my hand down over his chest, running my fingers through the short curls of hair. I feel completely overcome by his presence, his warm body against me, his scent surrounding me entirely.

"Just perfect," I gasp.

VIII.

He pulls me tighter against him, and I scoot as close as I can, enjoying the warmth radiating through his skin into mine. Warm or not, my nipples are still standing up proudly.

I move my hand over to the side, finding his nipple which is nearly hard enough to match mine. Softly I tug and pull at it, and caress its tip with my finger before propping myself up on my elbow.

I'm not patient or reserved like him; I want a taste straight away. He moans softly as I put my lips around his nipple and suck on it, letting my tongue caress him. Gently I take it between my teeth and tug a little.

My hand can't stay still either, rubbing against his temptingly soft flesh on his side and digging my fingertips in just a little more as I run my hand back down. While I continue to explore more of him, his back muscles relax under my touch. All tension seems to wash off him.

His hand travels down my own back and onto my ass, kneading and pulling me against his thigh.

"Help me please you," I demand. "Show me how you like it."

I slide my hand down, rubbing and fondling his belly before finding his very impressive, throbbing erection waiting for me just inside his boxer shorts. As soon as I touch him there, he trembles and groans.

The fact that he's hard again makes me smile. He's got stamina, I have to give him that.

He lets go of my arse and rests his hand on top of mine. He squeezes my fingers tightly around his hard cock. We both slide up and down the full length of it, before focussing just on the head for a couple of shallow strokes. Then, the same pattern repeats.

I lift myself up off the bed and push him onto his back while kneeling next to him. He complies without a fight, breathing loudly and groaning every time my hand pushes down on his long, thick shaft.

"I need your other hand," I whisper.

He runs it up over my thigh in response and I direct it to the moist spot on my thong. He seems to know just what I want, because he immediately starts to tease me, through the barely-there fabric. It sends shivers down my spine.

How is he so very good at this?

I lift myself, lean over him and bite and lick at his belly while still keeping a firm grasp on his manhood, stroking him in the same rhythm he had just showed me. Deep and hard a few times before switching to shallow and soft caresses.

Although his body reacts instantly to my affections, he doesn't appear to be ticklish. *Good.*

His finger slips past the thin strip of fabric of my thong, softly gliding over and outlining the skin folds leading up to my clitoris. I gasp for air when he moves his fingers back down and discovers my dripping wet entrance.

I release his cock from my firm grasp and run my hand up and down the soft skin on his inner thighs, first the left, then the right. I bend down deeper and scatter kisses all the way down his happy trail.

That's where I find my reward.

His finger has found its way inside of me, curled upwards and rubbing against the inside wall of my pussy. He doesn't fumble or hesitate. I ride his finger with short moves of my hips, directing his touch to achieve perfection inside of me.

I pout my lips and rub the head of his cock against them. Then, I let my tongue take over, licking him all around to get him nice and wet.

His finger almost goes limp—distracted—when I take his cock into my mouth for the first time.

I struggle to accept his full length, no matter how much I want to.

Is that his heartbeat I feel against my tongue?

His groans grow louder, more primal. Feeling his body writhe underneath my mouth, it's the most beautiful thing in the world. He's pushing himself up into me, spurring me on to go deeper and faster.

I take a deep breath and push down, willing myself not to gag.

"Oh fuck, I'm gonna..." He pants loudly.

I respond by sucking him harder once, then releasing him until his head barely remains inside my lips, before going down hard again. I keep going faster, again and again. His hips buckle up into me and his legs go stiff. His finger inside of me curls more, completely rigid while I feel his hot cum rush into my throat.

I'm right here with you...

I take his hand, forcing his finger out of me and show him how to rub my clit in a pattern that nearly makes me lose my mind. He's talented. It doesn't take him long to get it exactly right.

My second orgasm of the night hits me so hard I have to let his cock out slip of my mouth for fear of biting down.

I scream loudly and he fights the stranglehold of my hand on his to continue rubbing until my cries stop and I once more slump back onto the bed next to him.

An eternity passes before either of us have the energy to speak.

"That was... you're just..." He tries and fails to catch his breath. "Damn."

"Same back at ya," I say. "If you hadn't told me otherwise I could've bet you've done this loads of times before..."

"I suppose I may have had quite a while to research what to do... Just in case."

His admission makes me grin.

I strain to reach the light switch, but he immediately pulls me back and cuddles up to me from behind.

"Cath..." he starts. "You really don't mind?"

His breath tickles my neck and I close my eyes.

"Mind what?"

"Well, I guess traditionally I should've been more experienced. Taking the lead," he says.

"You're over thinking this. As I said, I wouldn't have

been able to guess. You've made me feel things I didn't know were possible," I respond.

"But we haven't, *you know*," he says.

"If I get to be your first, that would make me the luckiest girl in the world. Why would I mind that?" I whisper.

He kisses my neck and rests his face against mine. "You already are my first."

Hearing these words makes me want to pinch myself just to know I'm not dreaming.

"Just one thing. If I do anything that makes you uneasy, promise you'll tell me?" I ask.

He lets out a short laugh. "Sure thing, in that case can I put my shirt back on now?"

"Okay, anything *else*," I tease. "I'm not giving this up now!"

I reach behind me and place my hand on his side to make my point. *Perfection.*

He has no idea how tempted I am to turning around and taking a bite out of him.

His hand digs in between the mattress and my side, holding me firmly in place. I feel warm all over and not just because he's still burning up behind me. I'm warm *inside*, feeling a kind of happiness I haven't known in a long time. I feel like I've come home.

"So, nobody has ever made you feel like this? Not even guy-whose-clothes-I-was-wearing earlier?" I can't tell if he's teasing me or he's genuinely concerned.

"Especially not him," I respond.

"What happened?" he asks.

"Well, we were together for two years, but I guess I just didn't fit into what he wanted out of life," I say.

It's like I'm talking about someone else's life and not my own. Our relationship ended in heartbreak, but I let go of that sadness a long time ago.

"Sounds like he didn't know what he had," John says and kisses the special spot on my neck.

I wonder if it would be wise to elaborate.

"He hated himself," I say. "It was almost like he couldn't accept that I didn't, at least not when we were still together. I'm kind of glad he left when he did."

"Why do you say that?" John asks.

I release myself from his embrace and turn around to face him. It's too dark to see. I put my arms around his neck and wait for him to hold me once more.

"Because otherwise none of this would've happened," I say. "I would have never gone for this job. I wouldn't have met you."

My face is nestled comfortably against his shoulder.

"Sorry if I'm too clingy," I add. "I just don't feel like letting go yet."

He holds me even tighter.

"Not at all." He sighs. "I love this."

"Will you stay the night?" I ask the question without giving it much prior thought. Is it too much, too soon?

"I'll stay as long as you want me to."

He turns onto his back, pulling me along with him until my head rests against his shoulder. I could stay here forever, with one hand resting on his chest. He tucks the duvet around my shoulder to keep it in place.

My eyes close as I keep listening to his heartbeat. It's slowing, but so is mine.

IX.

It feels like I only closed my eyes a minute ago. When I open them again, it's already morning. Our glorious first night together feels like a distant dream, delicious as it was. John is nowhere to be seen.

Stretching and yawning a few times, I let my eyes adjust to the light filtering through the curtains and listen for any indicators of his presence elsewhere in the flat. *Nothing.*

It's chilly, as it should be in early December. Time to turn the thermostat up.

I get up and wrap the duvet throw around me while I search the room. His clothes are gone.

As I make my way down into the living room, I still see no sign of him. There's a note on the coffee table.

"Didn't want to wake you. Am visiting my parents today. See you tomorrow at work."

A bit strange that he just left like that, but maybe he was trying to be considerate by letting me sleep in. I try not to over think it.

After freshening up, I put on the robe he was wearing only yesterday. His scent still clings to the fabric, making me feel closer to him despite his absence.

My stomach growls, motivating me to make some breakfast.

Reflecting on last night, I can't believe how everything happened so quickly. But I'm not about to complain. John is amazing, I can't wait to see him again. I cuddle into the robe. No way am I taking this off anytime soon.

With a steaming mug of tea in hand, I make myself comfortable on the sofa. My phone is on the table next to the note.

Two new messages; both from Jason. Of course, he'll be keen to get a full update.

I dial his number straight away.

"Hey, darling, what's going on?" Jase answers. "I haven't heard from you in a while!"

"Oh, I'm great, actually." I settle deeper into the sofa cushions before continuing. "Just woke up and saw your messages. Let's just say yesterday was quite eventful."

"Oh really? Feel free to elaborate on that."

"I *finally* managed to hook up with John! And he's amazing, I couldn't have wished for anything better," I say.

"Hooked up eh? Hope you're not giving it up too easily. You want to keep him interested, don't you? Let's not fall into old patterns," Jase warns.

His concern makes me smile. Normally, I'd agree with his assessment. But this situation is wildly different. *John* is different.

"Don't think I'll have any trouble with that. So, let me tell you how it happened..." I start outlining everything that took place. From the note I'd left in his bag, to the unexpected visit in the middle of the night, right up to last night's party. I try to stick to the clean and wholesome version of the story, but throw in enough hints to keep Jase happy.

"Sweetheart, if I didn't know you better, I'd accuse of making things up. Such a sappy love story! I'm happy for you. Meanwhile, I also have some news of my own," he says, before telling me all about *his* date on Friday. Seems like we're both heading in similar directions with our love life. Finally!

After our catch-up session is over, I settle down in front of the TV for a bit.

I'm only half paying attention to the screen. Most of my thoughts are with John and desperately wanting to reach out. Just to let him know I'm thinking about him.

That's just needy, isn't it? We'll see each other tomorrow, anyway.

Jase does make a good point. I shouldn't make myself *too* available. Most men live for the hunt, not the having. And if this thing with John is meant to work out, I'd be stupid to fall into old traps. I don't want to lose myself in this relationship too soon, only to have him run for the hills. Nothing good ever comes out of stifling someone.

We could both use some time to process everything that has happened so far before seeing each other again.

This last realization helps to motivate me to find something else to occupy my Sunday afternoon. I start with a nice little meal, followed some of the video games I haven't played for a while. Too much time passes as I tire myself out shooting, stabbing and kicking at stuff on-screen.

By evening, I'm done in more ways than one. My

eyes burn and I'm exhausted. But John has been in the back of my mind throughout. And now that I'm properly *game over*, I again wonder what he's up to.

Before he came over on Friday night, we had started getting a little bit friendly at work, but there's still a lot I don't know. Surely after everything that's happened, it would be appropriate if I look him up online?

Opening Facebook on my phone, I type in his name. Damn, this is going to be more difficult than I anticipated. Scrolling through the various Jonathan/John Halls that Facebook has to offer, I feel like I'll never find him!

I switch to my laptop, so at least I can filter the results by location. Sure enough, the photo is unmistakably him, and my heart skips quite a few beats as I send him the request. Now all I can do is wait and wonder if he even checks this account or not. I've never seen him on his phone at the office. Does he even use Facebook at all?

Ten whole minutes pass while I'm still stalking the very few public parts of his profile. Two photographs, both gorgeous of course, even if the first is a bit outdated.

No status updates or other photo albums that I can see. His friend list seems to be private, so it provides no clues.

There's no response to my request yet and no link to send a message.

Studying the two photos again, I compare how he's changed over the years. The differences are subtle; in the most recent one he wears his hair slightly shorter, plus he obviously looks a couple of years older now. More office-proof.

But he doesn't appear too cheerful in either of them. He isn't really smiling, and his eyes look kind of cold.

I remember the look he gave me at the party, when he walked up to me with our drinks. Or the expression on his face when he stole glances at me over dinner. Last night I saw him look genuinely happy. That's how I want to see him again.

Once again, I'm excited about Monday morning, and work is the last thing on my mind.

X.

I enter the office even earlier than normal. It's largely quiet still.

There's no sign of John and for some reason my heart is pounding in my chest. I keep checking my phone, but he hasn't responded to the friend request I sent him either. I guess he's not active on social media then, which shouldn't be all that surprising. He doesn't appear very social at all.

By the time my watch says three minutes to nine, I decide to just go ahead and fetch some tea while I wait. I'm not entirely sure where to go from here. Jason's dating advice is still ringing in my ears.

At the same time, I'm completely taken over by John. I want nothing more but to spend every possible moment with him. Do stuff together, or just hang out at home.

Don't be so bloody clingy!

After placing one cup on his desk and sitting down taking a few careful sips of mine, I try to think of what he might like. He appears to be a bit of a geek, just like me. Video games, movies… Surely we'll find tons of things to agree on. Even our musical tastes seem similar enough. I don't know if he likes to go out to concerts, though. He's never really talked much about what he actually *does* in his spare time. Always a man of few words.

Five past nine.

I'd better get to work before people start to notice. Since we turned up at the Christmas party together, everyone will be scrutinizing my activities for weeks to come.

Finally, I see him come in. He avoids my gaze completely and just sits down in silence. He's as bleak as ever.

"Your tea might be lukewarm by now," I remark, studying his face.

He's unresponsive. Like nothing changed this weekend and we're strangers all over again.

Initial confusion gives way to blind panic. Everything was perfect when we went to sleep on Saturday night!

Was it something I said or did? *Was Jason right after all?*

Meanwhile he gets up and heads towards his favorite hide-out; the copier room.

I'm still dazed, but muster the courage to confront him anyway.

"John, what's wrong?" I ask, after closing the door behind me.

He's just standing there, staring at the floor while leaning against the copier with one hand.

"This weekend, it was a mistake," he says.

His words hurt like a slap in the face.

"What the hell do you mean, a mistake?" I argue. "If you weren't interested, you could've just said so, rather than sneaking off like a coward before I woke up and then acting like nothing happened!"

Rage has built up inside me and I'm having trouble controlling my volume.

"Well, you said you were single!" There it is. His eyes shoot daggers at me. "I should have known better."

"What are you talking about?" I hiss under my breath.

"Who the fuck is Jason? I didn't mean to spy, but your phone buzzed. I tried switching it off so the sound wouldn't disturb you. I saw his messages. *'Hi sweetheart,'* and so on. I'm not an idiot!" John glare at me for just a moment, then stares at the floor again.

Relief washes over me straight away.

"Jesus, that's all?" I take a few steps towards him, but he refuses to look at me. His expression remains tense.

"John, listen. We grew up together." I try to take his hand but he pulls away. "He's my best friend. Plus, he's gay!"

"Oh fuck," he whispers.

Just like that, his whole demeanor makes a U-turn and now he just looks defeated. I try to pull him towards me by his shoulders, but he barely reacts.

"I'm so sorry, Cath. I assumed... seeing the message and his picture next to it... Every one of my instincts screamed at me that this thing we had couldn't be real."

"Look at me," I say, guiding his face towards me with my hand.

When he makes eye contact, it becomes obvious how betrayed he must have felt. He's a mess.

"I see how his messages would have made you feel that way. That's just the way he talks. And I should've told you about him, but it's all been so sudden we haven't got the chance to get to know each other yet."

I get up onto the balls of my feet and put both arms around him tightly. He doesn't reciprocate my smile.

"Jason, my boyfriend. Ick! He's like a big brother to me," I add.

He soon starts to relax under my touch and sure enough his arms find their way around me as well. He sighs, bending down so I don't have to tiptoe anymore. His face pressed against my neck, we stand like this for what feels like ages.

It's fine, just a misunderstanding. Growing pains are to be expected in any relationship, especially this early on.

John has been hurt in the past. It's obvious that he has some baggage. As do I.

My heartbeat slows to a more normal pace, until the door swings open, and scares the hell out of me. We jump apart, but it's too late to make this look casual.

"What the...!" Dick calls out. "Cath, a word in my office, if you don't mind!"

PART III.

I.

"Cath, I'm sorry it had to come to this, but I'm sure you're aware of the reason I've asked you to come in."

Dick gives me a look which suggests he's enjoying this more than he should. He closes the vertical blinds and sits down on his chair, hands folded on the desk in front of him.

"I have some idea, yes." I squint slightly, but maintain eye contact.

I cannot get fired! My heart is pounding, but I'm not about to back down without a fight. He might have caught John and me together, but we weren't *doing* anything.

"When I hired you, I made it clear that your initial three months would be on a probationary basis. I don't need to tell you that there have been concerns."

"If it's not too much to ask, I'd love specific examples of when my work has been lacking?" My tone is curt and I continue to stare at the smug expression on his face.

"It's not so much the quality of your work. You've only just undergone your training, after all. But you cannot deny that there have been issues with your attitude and efforts to fit into the team here." Dick adjusts his hands slightly.

He seems to think he is handling this with the finesse of a seasoned politician.

He's wrong.

"Assuming you're considering disciplinary action of some sort, shouldn't there be a representative from HR present?" I change the topic.

His face hardens.

"As your direct manager, I have the authority to hold performance appraisals without involvement from HR if I feel it is the appropriate path to take."

"I didn't realize this was a previously scheduled appraisal. I've not been given time to prepare." It's obvious that Dick isn't enjoying my responses. The involuntary twitch in the corner of his mouth is a dead giveaway.

"Cath, let's cut the crap, alright? The reason I've called you in here is that I am willing to give you one last chance to adjust your attitude. I can't have people in this team who won't give it their all."

He gets up and leans against the side of his desk, too close for comfort. My heart is racing again and I'm not sure whether to run or fight. My bank statement at the end of every month doesn't fail to remind me how badly I need this job.

"You may not know it, but I've seen you look at me from across the office," he says.

My mouth falls open but I can't find the words to respond. How deluded can he be?

Meanwhile he just looks down at me, enjoying the inherent position of power he has while I'm still sitting down. And the view from above seems to please him as well.

"What is it that you want, exactly?" I sneer.

My question is quite unnecessary, I suspect that I already know.

He leans down and catches a lock of my hair between his fingers, pushing it behind my ear. His face is only inches away from my ear when he speaks again.

"Look, I don't know what game you're playing, hanging around that fat bastard, John… But I'm not going to play along forever. Enough is enough."

I'm holding on to the armrests of the chair in a vice-like grip, while trying not to shiver. This is not fucking happening! The raw emotions caused by my earlier quarrel with John flare back up. Fury washes over me.

"You make a lot of assumptions, Richard! I am not now and not ever—"

He pushes me back down into the chair just as I try to get up. I feel sick having his face so close to mine.

"You're such a cock tease, you know that? If you value your career, you will shut up and do what is asked of you. Don't doubt for a minute that I can't make a few phone calls and ruin any chance of finding another job in this industry. Forget about any letter of recommendation. And the same goes for your *lover boy* out there." Despite the low volume, his voice sounds utterly grim.

"Who do you think they'll believe, the manager with years of impeccable performance? Or the new girl who's apparently sleeping her way around the office floor?" His fingers dig painfully into my arms when he makes this final point.

Fleeing is no longer an option, so the instinct to fight takes over.

"I don't give a fuck who they'll believe!" I scream. "Get your filthy hands off me right now!"

The door crashes open and interrupts my outburst.

"What the fuck do you think you're doing!" John looks furious as he charges up to Dick.

"I... we were just talking." Dick flinches backwards, giving me room to escape. "How did you? I thought I'd locked..."

It's surreal, like a slow-motion action sequence in a movie.

John looks powerful as he towers over Dick, who's still in shock at the interruption. With his shoulders and back straightened, John is quite a bit taller as well as broader, obviously. It's no contest.

Dick goes down with a single punch, accompanied by a barrage of curses and insults. He knocks over the dustbin next to his desk along the way. An empty coke can rolls across the floor and stops at my feet. The whole situation is so bizarre it's almost funny.

Almost, but not quite.

I have caught a glimpse of John's temper already this morning. He's a force to be reckoned with. But where he had controlled his anger with me, Dick has no such luck. The calm and quiet John everyone's been seeing at work is just a front. Reality is a lot more complicated.

As scary as it is, I can't stand by and let things get further out of hand.

I force myself to my feet and approach the two of

them. John is so tense; he doesn't even react when I place my hand on his shoulder to try and pull him away. Instead, he continues to stare down at Dick with balled fists, ready to make another move.

"John," I whisper, with a tremor in my voice. "Please stop."

When my hand touches his, he seems to snap out of it a little. Finally, he unclenches his fist and threads his fingers through mine. When he faces me, his eyes are still burning with rage, even though his expression has calmed slightly.

"Are you okay? Did he hurt you?" he asks.

"Yeah, fine. Let's go? Please?"

It's obvious he's far from done with Dick, but he still does as asked. Both of us come into view of all the prying eyes that have gathered outside the office. The shock is clearly written on all their faces. Sharon is the most notable exception; she gives me a look that suggests she's already decided my guilt.

Nobody dares to say a word. They wait until we're well out of the way before apprehensively entering Dick's office to check on him.

In the lift, John turns towards me and puts his arms around me. He's quiet, but he's obviously still seething.

In the safety of his embrace, I start to come to terms with everything. From the moment Dick summoned me into his office, there was never going to be a positive outcome to all of this. Perhaps I sealed our fate with my taunts at the Christmas party itself.

We can't work here anymore.

We have been together for mere days and everything is unravelling around us already. Are we doomed?

I close my eyes and try to focus on calming my breaths. Tears sting, but I don't want to let them out. John's warm hands on my back give me goose bumps.

The lift doors open but we don't stir. A minute or so later I hear them close again.

"I'm so sorry. I should've never let you go in there by yourself."

"You didn't have a choice. How could anyone predict that it was going to turn out like this?" My voice sounds flat and empty, I'm still trying my best not to cry.

"Bullshit. You asked me not to leave you alone with that asshole. I should have been there!"

I pull back and hold his face in my hands. He refuses to look directly at me but I can see tears in his eyes as well. It breaks my heart that he blames himself. That's the last thing we need right now.

"Stop it. You kept me safe. Nothing actually happened in there and it's all thanks to you."

He shakes his head.

"You saved me. Thank you." I stand on tiptoe and kiss him on the lips but still, no reaction. "It's not your fault, it's his!"

"Oh but it is. He wouldn't even have called you in for the meeting if it wasn't for my idiotic behavior this morning. I fucked up. How can you just stand there and tell yourself that I saved you, when only this same morning I was ready to call you a liar and a cheat!"

"That was a misunderstanding! You don't know if he'd already decided to call me into his office today and that's why he was looking for us in the first place."

As much as I try to stop them, a couple of tears escape and run down my face.

"My stupidity put you in harm's way. How do I fix this?" he whispers.

I kiss him again through my tears.

"You could start by not pushing me away now. By taking me home."

He nods in silence.

I press the button to open the doors again and we make our way out of the building.

It feels permanent.

II.

His place is nearest, so that's where we go.

By the time we reach it, his mood hasn't improved and I'm exhausted. It feels like it has been a long day, even if it's only ten-thirty.

The disaster zone in his living room that I remember from Saturday has changed significantly. All of the mess, the reminders of his struggles, are tidied away.

I sit down on the sofa and stare at nothing. He wanders off somewhere, but I haven't got the energy to go after him. He's obviously still upset and although I tried already, I'm not sure how to make it better.

The seriousness of everything that has happened is starting to sink in. If John hadn't come in when he did, who knows how far Dick would've gone? Sure, I got angry enough to make a scene. But physically, I couldn't have done a damn thing. He had all the power, and I had none.

I had always picked up a creepy vibe from him and he obviously has no concept of personal space. But somehow, I still thought he was mostly harmless. I'm such an idiot for not catching on sooner.

He might have forced himself on me. I'd like to think I would have tried to stop him. But would I, really? Could I have done anything at all? My whole life, I've never been in a physical fight. I've always had Jason to look out for me.

The ease with which Dick kept me confined in that chair shook me to my core. I'm ashamed at my own weakness as well as naivety.

And now, I have no doubt that we're both jobless. Half of the office saw or heard it when John hit him. But nobody witnessed what Dick was trying to do behind closed doors. This could get ugly, what if John gets done for assault? Any justification John could possibly have is just 'he said, she said'.

Worst of all is John is taking it personally, as if it's his fault.

It's all just too much to deal with. I hide my head in my hands and tears start to flow freely at last. I'm too tired to hold anything back anymore and I'm reduced to a sobbing mess. My mascara starts to stain my hands and my nose starts to drip uncontrollably.

But it's nowhere near stopping as despair claws at my throat and lungs. Loud sobs make way for silent tears, until I clam up completely. Then I feel a warm hand on my shoulder and movement next to me.

"Hey! Please don't cry!" John says.

"Sorry..." I'm choked, but there is no stopping the flood.

His arm wraps around me tightly and I curl up against him. My outburst has brought on a splitting headache, which threatens to blind me. I've never been a good crier.

I press my face into his chest and notice he's changed his clothes. The white office shirt he had on earlier has made way for a dark hoodie. That's all I can make out through the blur.

With my face pressed against the soft fabric and his hand caressing my hair, I start to slowly calm down again.

"I just— I feel so helpless. I didn't want to get you into trouble!" I sniffle. "And now..."

"Don't be silly, the only one who's in trouble is that twat Richard."

"I really thought he was just a bit creepy. It never occurred to me that he would take things so far. I'm so stupid." I sigh.

"Stop, it's not your fault," he says. "I never figured it out until now, but in hindsight he may have caused similar trouble before. I'm going to ensure that it ends here."

I straighten myself to look him in the face. His expression is grim and determined. He's not going to back down from this.*My hero.*

"What are you planning to do?" I blink a few times, hoping to unstick my wet lashes.

"We're going to report the matter to HR. By the book. He will try to deny it all, but that's not going to help him."

I sit quietly for a minute, thinking it all through.

"But you still punched him," I say.

He shrugs. "He was trying to attack you first. I overheard you screaming at him to stop."

Suddenly I can't help but grin at John. "Did you see his face though, when you came in? He looked so scared, I thought he was going to faint!"

He returns my smile and attempts to wipe some of the messy, smudged tears off my face.

"To be honest, I wasn't paying attention to his face that much. Just enough to get a good aim of course."

"Of course." A smile still plays on my lips.

But it does not last as I look down past the wet tear stains I've left behind on his clothes and spot his right hand sitting on his thigh. I carefully pick it up to inspect his reddened knuckles.

"Does it hurt?" I ask, still looking at the bruised skin.

He opens and closes his fist a few times.

"Just a little sore," he replies. "Should be okay in a day or two."

"Don't tell me you've done this sort of thing before!" I say.

"It's been a few years." He grins. "Let's just say people stopped picking on me when I discovered certain advantages to having a bigger build."

I get up from the sofa before sitting down on his lap, facing him. Both hands resting on his chest, I lean in for a kiss.

"I'm impressed," I whisper, before kissing his neck.

"That's the secret, is it? So, back in the day when I couldn't get a date to save my life, all I had to do was punch someone?" he remarks dryly.

"Fair point. Guess I was already impressed before and this just amplified it," I say.

He runs both his hands over my sides, squeezing me gently. I respond by shifting closer, our torsos brushing together.

His breath tickles my throat, and puts my whole body on edge. The sensation gets even more intense when I feel his lips on me. Soft kisses follow my jaw line and travel the side of my neck down to my shoulder.

I'm helpless, held firmly in place with my knees spread wide and wetness soaking through my underwear. All I can do is savor his touch on my ass and the gentle nibbling of his lips around my collar bone. I can hardly catch my breath, and run my hands through his hair. I tug at it just enough to pull his head back.

"You have no idea how much I want you," I whisper in his ear. "It's all I can think about."

His accelerated breaths betray a similar thought. He wants what I want. His eyes are ready to burn a hole in me. He pulls me in and his lips hungrily seek out mine again.

We kiss without any playfulness or attempts to tease. There is an urgency in our movements, one that must be fulfilled or else we might lose our minds. It's like even the air is buzzing with excitement. Until there's something else, *actually* buzzing and distracting us.

The moment is disturbed and we both turn our heads towards the origin of the noise. His phone.

My arousal subsides as I'm reminded of our terrible reality.

"What if it's—" I look at John, who immediately turns serious as well.

"The office?" he concludes.

I rush up to fetch the phone. The weakness in my knees and the cold sensation in my crotch are stark reminders of how quickly things change.

"Hello? Speaking," John answers.

"Yes, indeed I took her home because she was obviously shaken up. She wants to make a formal complaint against Richard." He nods a few times as the person on the other end speaks.

"I understand... Yes I can hold."

He looks up at me.

"Gary wants a word with me. I'm going to give him a full account of what happened. He's a decent enough guy. Don't worry, okay?"

I struggle to remember who Gary is, but then it comes back to me. The elusive guy in the office upstairs. Upper management. Gary is Dick's immediate boss.

"Right," I say. "Hey, mind if I use your shower? Unless you need me to talk to him too..."

"Yeah, go ahead. It would be best if you tell your side of it in a formal meeting," John says.

As I make my way to the bathroom, my earlier worries and exhaustion are trying to make a comeback. Today has been way too much.

In the bathroom, I can't find the clean towels, so I borrow his from the rail. The strong stream of water looks so inviting. A hot shower should do me a world of good.

My reflection in the mirror makes me chuckle. My God, these must be the worst panda eyes in the history of mankind. While the water warms up, I do my best to clean up my face.

I get into the shower, close my eyes and wait for all

the negativity to be washed away. But it doesn't seem to be working and I still feel faint.

Perhaps a little massage… I take the shower head off the holder and sit down in the tub with my legs stretched out ahead of me. The warm stream of water fizzles against my chest and down my stomach. *That's the ticket.*

I've always loved long showers. How the water rushes against my skin and makes me tingle and relax at the same time. I could do with some distraction from all the negativity.

With my eyes closed, I remember how I straddled John on the sofa. How his body felt, tightly pressed against me. So tempting... And that look on his face.

A soft moan escapes my lips when I let my hands glide over my breast. My skin is slippery, wet, as is my pussy. I direct the flow of the shower head against my nipple and it tickles deliciously. Then I move the stream down and let it massage my tense abdomen.

I know I must have release, quickly, or else this cloud will hang over me for the rest of the day.

With the strong stimulation from the shower directed at my clit and my hand keeping me spread wide, my orgasm is swift and intense.

III. JOHN

After telling Gary all about this morning's events, I'm confident that things will go in our favor. He never liked Richard much, he confesses. Found him to portray a less than professional image around the office.

Gossip does travel.

Clearly, this situation will be used to further Gary's own agenda. Dick was an old hire inherited from Gary's predecessor; he'll want to choose somebody new to take his place.

What do I care? As long as it works out for Cath.

In any case, we're free until the meeting in the morning. Richard will get suspended with immediate effect. That's standard procedure in cases like this.

If I am to believe Gary, nothing will happen to me. But I'm not counting on anything before he and HR make their decision tomorrow. Either way, I'm not going to worry about it now. Not when I have Cath here to take care of.

The battery of my phone is getting low after the call, so I head into the bedroom to look for my charger. When I pass the bathroom, I can clearly hear the shower. The door has popped open just a little, as it usually does, thanks to the faulty lock.

I don't want to intrude, but I cannot resist the temptation of catching a glimpse.

The sight of her stops me in my tracks. Steam rises and swirls around her as she's leaning back in the tub. I fail to remember what I was doing or where I was going.

She has her eyes closed. Her nearly black wet hair has stuck to her delicate shoulders, framing her beautiful face. Her perfectly formed breasts stand proud and nipples harden visibly while she caresses and teases herself.

She then moves the shower head down below out of my view. The resulting moans and rapid movements of her hand tell me all I need to know.

Before the phone interrupted us, I had been ready for anything. I could clearly see her need for me. Her eyes begged for affection. For comfort. Her body was calling out to me and I knew I must answer.

The first time, in her bed, pleasuring her came so naturally. The taste and feel of her skin made me forget who I am. I felt like a real man. Powerful and capable, as she squirmed underneath me. That one experience gave me the confidence to take things further.

When she took over on Saturday, I knew that she would always have me wrapped around her finger.

I want her so much my cock starts aching uncomfortably. But I dare not disturb the beautiful scene in front of me.

Next time...

I finally understand why some people are caught fucking outside in the rain. Barely hidden behind a parked car and allowing others to look on. You get to a point of no return, where you don't care who's looking. The only thing that matters is *having* her and making her scream.

Her eyebrows crinkle together in that little frown she makes when she's close and my own hand moves furiously to a similar end. Another moan escapes her lips while I wonder if being inside her would feel similar to being sucked off.

That thought is all I need.

Leaning against the wall, just out of view from the partially open door, I try my best to catch my breath. She's stirring inside, having turned off the shower. I couldn't help but watch her, but now that it's done, I feel a pang of guilt. After this morning, the last thing she needs is another guy creeping on her.

I force myself to move along and put that phone on charge which I've been holding on to all along. There should be some tissues around here somewhere.

Only moments after I finish cleaning up, Cath walks in. My dark blue towel is wrapped tightly around her body. Her face is fresh and she's even more beautiful for it.

"Sorry, I hope you don't mind I borrowed this?" she smiles, clearly more relaxed now.

With every step, the towel opens slightly, exposing her entire thigh up to her hip. It's still hard to believe she's actually here with me.

And I can't get enough of the way she looks at me. She doesn't just look, she *sees*.

"I don't feel like wearing my office clothes again." Her eyes wander from me over to the wardrobe.

I step up and open its doors, exposing the chaos

inside.

"Don't think anything would work," I say.

Once again, I'm reminded of how mismatched we are and it's awkward. Any other couple might be able to share sweats for example without too much trouble.

She takes an old black T-shirt from one of the shelves.

"This should do," she remarks after holding it up to herself.

Before I'm able to get a word out, she drops the towel. I can't breathe, only stare, while she covers her damp, naked body with the T-shirt. Then she gives me a peck on the cheek. "Thanks, babe."

She walks off, with the towel now draped over her arm.

I'm left behind, watching the suggestion of her shapely behind swaying side to side underneath the loose cotton. The T-shirt covers her halfway down her thigh and even though it's huge and has been washed one too many times, she still makes it look sexy somehow.

IV.

The look on his face was priceless.

I have never been self-conscious. My body isn't perfect, but that's okay. It's the only one I've got, so I'm determined to enjoy it.

And the looks he keeps giving me are like an addiction. It's taken me long enough to get his attention initially and now I want him speechless again and again. More than anything, I guess I want him to know I'm his.

The incident at work showed me one thing above all, he may be shy, insecure about a lot of things, but he's the sort of man I've always dreamed of: sensitive on the inside, but strong and protective when he needs to be. He won't think twice when push comes to shove.

This part of his character speaks to me on a primal level.

I was forced to grow up at a young age. Even before Mum left and Jason's family took me in. My self-reliance was always a point of pride for me. And as much as the situation with Dick made me doubt myself, I am kind of enjoying being able to lean on someone new.

Cliché perhaps, but there is no aphrodisiac quite like being rescued. I wasn't lying when I told John that I was impressed.

Even now that the immediate danger is over, he's still taking care of me by handling the fallout. I'm so grateful for it.

Now that I've relaxed as well as found my much-needed release, I realize that I'm starving. The fridge in the kitchen has nothing much in it. There are some ready meals in the freezer, along with the obligatory bag of frozen peas every household seems to have. Nothing appeals.

I find a bunch of take-away menus on the counter and start leafing through them when John comes up behind me.

"Hungry?" he asks.

"Yeah, how about you?"

"Oh, I could eat something."

"I'd love to cook something nice, if I had the ingredients," I muse.

A repayment of sorts; a chance for *me* to take care of *him* again after everything he's done for me today.

He puts his arms around my waist and I lean back against him.

"Sorry, groceries haven't really been on my mind lately," he says.

"Don't tell me you've just been eating all this instant rubbish?" I turn around, frowning.

"I'm afraid so." He brushes a strand of hair out of my face and smiles.

"That won't do! How about this, assuming you have bread somewhere, we'll just have a sandwich now and then I'll cook you something decent for dinner?"

"I'd love that," he says and gives me a kiss on my forehead.

He fetches a loaf of bread from a tall cupboard I

wouldn't have thought to check.

"I just realized, I've never seen you have lunch at work. What sort of sandwiches do you like?" I ask.

"I'm not picky. There's ham in the fridge."

Our little meal doesn't take long. I make a few sandwiches and we eat them standing up in the kitchen.

Preparing to change, I get my clothes from the bathroom.

"Your bathroom door keeps opening on its own," I remark upon coming back to the living room.

"Yeah, I'm aware." The blush creeping across his face tells me everything I need to know.

It's quite an effort, but I just about manage to keep a straight face and stay quiet. Instead I grab a pen and paper and head back into the kitchen.

Let's see what all I need for dinner.

V.

The small supermarket just around the corner is surprisingly well stocked and I manage to tick everything off my list. It's not going to be a gourmet meal, but at least an improvement compared to the contents of his freezer.

I've always liked to cook, but it gets so boring when there is nobody to appreciate the end result. John will, though. He looked absolutely ecstatic when I made him breakfast on Saturday. Same thing just now when I put together the simplest sandwich in the world.

It's quite adorable.

When I get back to his place an hour later, he's sitting on the sofa, writing on a notepad. He looks up to greet me and his eyes linger on certain features of mine just a little longer than others. I wonder what's on his mind but I don't get the chance to ask.

"I was just writing down a few things for tomorrow. Topics to be mentioned, complaints," he says.

"Right." I walk back over to him after leaving the food in the kitchen. "What have you got so far?"

All the events from this morning, as well as some of the unpleasantness at the Christmas party are noted down already. There is a glaring omission, though.

"Remember the other week when I asked you not to leave me alone with him? I never had the chance to tell you why," I say.

I tell him about Dick cornering me by the drinks machine, until Sharon appeared and I could make my escape.

John's face hardens in a frown.

"Why didn't you say something then? That's completely out of line!"

"I didn't expect he would go further than that! I just thought he was creepy," I explain with a shrug.

John shakes his head and adds it to his notes. I recognize the same expression on his face from this morning and decide to give him some space to calm down. Otherwise, I might just panic and say something to make it even worse.

It's kind of nerve wracking, knowing he's frustrated because of something I did, or didn't do as is the case now. As a result, it takes me a fair while to locate everything I need to cook.

But once I get started, I forget about everything else. Slicing, chopping and frying, it's so very relaxing. And while the sauce simmers away, I turn around to find John leaning against the door frame, smiling.

"Been watching me long?" I ask.

"Sadly, I missed the bit at the beginning."

"I hope you like pasta," I say.

"Who doesn't?" he responds.

We move back into the living room, leaving the sauce to simmer for a while.

I read through the notes he's made; he's added something.

"Who's this? Tracy?" I ask, pointing at the last item

on the list.

"Richard's previous mistake," John says.

He tells me about an incident a year ago, where a girl named Tracy joined the Accounts department. Unfortunately for her, Dick noticed her one day in the hallway. Things appeared to end badly after she refused him. John never knew how badly, only that she left abruptly one day, never to return.

While I was out at the shops, he managed to look her up online. She told him the whole story of what happened to her and she's happy to help. John set up a separate meeting for her with Gary tomorrow.

Things are starting to look up. I sort of knew Dick was bluffing in his office when he said nobody would believe me. But I do know how it appears; John and me going to the Christmas party together and then him storming into a meeting in Dick's office. One might think we orchestrated the whole series of events just to cause trouble and force Dick out.

Corroboration from a third party—that changes everything.

"Thank you," I mumble, still looking down at the notepad.

"What are friends for," John says.

"Hmm yeah, we're not just friends though, are we?" I say, looking back up.

"We are whatever you want us to be." He looks uneasy.

I know I'm putting him on the spot, but it's an important question. And I suppose it's also just a little bit amusing, watching him fret over where this conversation is going.

"I need to know what I am to you," I insist.

He takes a deep breath and leans back into the sofa. Then he laughs nervously.

"They never tell you how hard this is! I've never been great with people, especially not girls."

"Am I just some girl to you?" I ask with a wicked smile.

"No! Not some girl. I suppose you're the one that stayed when others ran," he says.

I squeeze his hand.

"There are no wrong answers, I just need to know what you think about everything. You worry too much," I say.

He looks at me and pauses a little.

"You are..."

I wait, growing nervous myself. He softly runs his thumb over the back of my hand and my heart jumps.

"When I'm around you, I feel like everything I've ever worried about is meaningless. I'm insanely jealous of every man you've ever had in your life before and at the same time grateful that they indirectly let you end up here, with me.

"And to think that that asshole, Richard, tried to hurt you... I saw red. If you hadn't stopped me, who knows what I would've done to him.

"I wish that I could be enough for you, that whatever it is that makes you like me doesn't go away. I really am not used to being around people much. I realized it can be hard to live with someone when Julie stayed with me for a while. But with you it's different... I just don't want you to leave.

"When I went home on Sunday morning, it was the hardest thing because I felt like a part of me was left behind. But I felt so betrayed and knew if what I suspected was true, staying would break me."

He smiles awkwardly and looks down at our hands. I'm dazed by his confession, don't doubt a word of it. When I pushed him just now, I never expected such a detailed reply.

I owe him the same amount of honesty, at least.

"John," I whisper.

"I have something to confess. I knew some details about what happened with Julie because Amanda told me. And it pissed me off so much, because I knew you deserved way better.

"Every day you came into work and it was obvious how hurt you were. All I wanted was to make you smile. I wished so much that you would see my intentions.

"I love spending time together, and I want to know everything about you. I wish for a lot more than friendship."

He's quiet. I wonder if I freaked him out? But if so, he doesn't show it. He simply pulls me closer and rests his face against my hair.

"Is this real?" he asks finally.

"It feels real to me," I answer. "But don't think saying a bunch of sweet things gets you off the hook for peeping on me in the shower."

"The door was open!" he protests.

I chuckle.

"Accidentally! So, were you *just* watching?" I say, playfully poking him in the side.

"Were you *just* showering?"

"Fair point," I say, snuggling against him and replaying everything he's just said in my head.

"Oh, for that list." I point at the notepad. "I almost forgot because at the time I was too preoccupied.

"But during my job interview, he spent more time looking at my boobs than my face; I guess you should add that."

"What?! For fuck's sake, Cath." John lets out an exasperated sigh.

"Oops?"

"It's a miracle you've made it this far in one piece! Why on earth did you take the job when it started off that way already?" He doesn't sound too pissed off this time at least.

"You're not going to like the answer," I say.

"Oh?"

"Money played a big part. But in truth, I was too distracted by the sight of you through the window to think about his sleazy behavior," I explain.

For a few minutes, there is no need for further conversation. We've got our arms around each other and I feel like this is exactly how things should be. In a weird way being so close is relaxing, but my heart is pounding relentlessly in my chest all the same.

"Crap, I'd better check on the food," I say, rushing to get to the kitchen.

VI.

I somehow made it look easy, running into the kitchen to rescue a forgotten dish on the stove and turning it into something edible.

He has a way of distracting me just with his presence. I can't believe I'm here in his house, after all we've been through.

Throughout the process of finally boiling the pasta, before plating it all up, he kept eyeing me. Almost in awe, as if I was performing some kind of magic. I wonder if it was the knowledge that I'm not wearing anything underneath this T-shirt, or for another reason. Maybe I'll gather the courage to ask later.

Now that we're done and the dishes have been cleared away, we're back on the sofa, exploring the eclectic, weird and wonderful collection of music on his phone. One ear bud each, we take turns to scroll through the song list and pick something.

"I love this song," I say, upon selecting The Beatles, 'While my Guitar Gently Weeps'. He takes the phone from my hand and puts it next to him on the sofa. His fingers run over mine, exploring the indents between my knuckles, following the veins on the back of my hand down to my wrist before turning my hand over and softly caressing my palm and fingers.

The combination of his soft touch and the beautiful tune in my ear turns me to mush. I try to compose myself but it's no use, I'm hopelessly lost for words and my heart rate is up exponentially.

He lets go of my hand and runs his fingers through my hair. Then he guides my face in his direction. He looks at me with such tenderness, I forget to breathe.

I wait, partially because I'd love to find out where he wants to take this, but mostly because I'm simply frozen. He comes closer, with his hand slipping around my neck. I love the taste of his lips; the care with which he kisses me.

Finally, I manage to react, even if my breathing is still letting me down. I grab hold of his hoodie and lift myself towards him. As focussed as he is, I am impatient. His arm wraps around my waist while he shifts around and leans back against the armrest of the sofa with me against him.

Fully on top of him, I'm intoxicated. His hands on my back and his tongue against mine. It feels like we're a couple of over-eager teenagers, unable to let go of our first taste of each other. We make out as if nothing else matters.

It occurs to me that ordinarily my comparison would be quite casual, but in this case it's not far off the truth. Although not by choice, it feels as if he saved up all this passion, just for me.

He didn't fully spell it out earlier, but I understood that he had fallen for me as hard as I had for him. It's all such a beautiful coincidence.

With the music now on shuffle, the mood changes on its own. From the beginning of Tim Minchin's 'Peace

Anthem', I start to giggle uncontrollably in his mouth.

"This song..." I chuckle, it's infectious.

"Stop laughing, you're tickling me!" He grins.

I remove the earphone and attempt to keep a straight face while sitting up. After leaving the phone on the table, I turn my focus back to him underneath me. The way he looks up at me with his eyes expectantly wide makes me forget my ill-timed sense of humor.

His hands start to caress my bare thighs, while he continues to look into my eyes. He has to be the most patient man alive because it takes me seemingly forever to stop staring and actually move.

"I wish you could see what I see right now," I whisper.

I lean down and unzip his hoodie in one smooth gesture. He tries to reach for a kiss but I'm a fraction of an inch too far away and continue to savor the view.

"Oh yeah, what's that?" he asks.

I momentarily break eye contact, noticing the dark blue T-shirt my actions have just exposed. Or rather, I'm noticing what's underneath, because in all our excitement it has ridden up a bit.

"A dream I've had over and over," I say.

My hand reaches for the side of his belly, caressing him and lying back down against him for more kisses. I can feel him shiver, making me want to play with more of him. His side first, then reaching upwards under the stretched out T-shirt and running my fingertips softly over his chest.

Just like Saturday night, I can't get enough of how he

feels. Then, I relied only on touch. now I get to enjoy the desire in his eyes as well. Looks can't kill but they can definitely set you alight. I think he's feeling the effects as much as I am.

There is something rather special about being with a big man. The sensuality of it, the softness I can caress or dig my fingers into. It causes a kind of sensory overload unmatched by anything else I know.

The prospect of feeling his whole body against mine with nothing in the way has me panting for air. I simply cannot understand how anyone would prefer hard muscle over all this.

Impatient and greedy, I let my hands run over him freely. He doesn't seem concerned anymore when I push his T-shirt up as far as it will go. Instead he's focused on enjoying more of my body through what little I'm wearing.

I'm glad he's letting me see this time, his almost flawless skin with some brown hair along the center of his torso. It's tragic how shy he is about this, possibly even a bit ashamed. When he's so irresistibly beautiful to me.

Would he believe me if I told him? I'm not sure, but I've made it my mission to show him. Again and again.

I love the fact that when I lean down, his body is so accommodating and adjusts to mine. And when I sit back up to look at him, his short, excited breaths look more obvious; amplified even.

Underneath me, the rough fabric of his jeans brushes against my most sensitive parts with every move he makes. All of it makes me giddy, and wet all over again. I struggle to remember the last time I've lusted this much after one guy, multiple times on any given day.

Probably because that's never happened before.

He can't stay still and neither can I. I ache for his hands, his lips, but more than that I need to be one with him. Never have I wanted something so much and been forced to wait. Normally a guy might want in my pants before I get the chance to change my mind.

He grinds up against me and again a bulge in his jeans hit me where it's needed the most.

"John, why do you torture me?"

I cling on to him with one hand and let the other travel downwards. The moment I touch his crotch he groans loudly into my ear.

Sitting up again, I swiftly remove my T-shirt. He glides his hands up my sides and carefully cups my breasts. His face already looks flushed and eyes are glazed over. But I want to see more desire in him, more pleasure! I aim for total desperation to match my own.

Perhaps then, I'll get to break through every last one of his barriers.

"I love how you know to touch me just right," I whisper.

My own hand once more explores his hardness through his jeans. I try to open the button, but it's too tight, forcing me to struggle with both hands. As soon as I unzip him, he's held back only by the soft cotton of his boxers.

I must remember to tell him I love boxers on a man.

On him.

Again I lean down and rub against him, enjoying how he completes every contour of my body, and nibble and lick any exposed skin within reach. Warmth emanating from his skin soothes mine and yet gives me goose bumps at the same time.

Another groan escapes him when I slip my hand in and squeeze his cock hard before freeing it completely. His breaths caress my shoulder in short bursts and his previously expert touch on my back and ass has turned erratic.

"I want..." he says.

"Tell me,"

His cock feels bigger than ever in my hand and I'm incredibly tempted to take him past the point of no return. But I don't; I pause for his response instead.

"Could we...?" He looks helpless.

I dive down to suck and nibble on his earlobe before speaking.

"Do you want to *fuck*?" I whisper.

He grabs my ass hard and bucks his hips upwards, into me. Seems I've succeeded.

"We're wearing too much," I say.

Pushing myself up with both hands on his chest, I get off him to take off my panties. He looks a little bewildered but follows my example and gets off the sofa as well. His jeans drop to the floor, and he takes a step out of them.

"Bedroom." I tug at his hand and he follows.

VII.

Inside, I turn towards him and reach for his boxers, sliding them all the way down. His T-shirt has fallen and covered him again while walking, I reach underneath to continue caressing him. He gets the hint straight away and takes it off.

We kiss like our lives depend on it.

"Lie down for me," I say, our lips only millimeters apart.

He does as asked and I get on top of him. Little beads of sweat have formed on his forehead. He looks at me apologetically when I touch his not-so-hard-anymore cock.

"I want to feel you inside me," I whisper, "I have done from the moment I first saw you."

Upon guiding his hand to my pussy, I start to caress and squeeze his balls. He closes his eyes and breathes deeply.

"Do we need a—you know—a condom?" he asks.

I shake my head. "I'm on the pill."

It's a revelation that I don't have to think about this too much. I'll be his first. There is nothing else to worry about.

I cover his chest with kisses and he fists my hair. He loves the extra attention I'm giving to his nipples and gently nudges me back when I try to move away.

I'm happy to give him more of what he wants,

sucking and licking him, feeling him quiver every time my tongue hits him just right. When I look up, I notice he's watching me.

His fingers tease me, slick with my own wetness and I cry out for more. My hand tightens around his cock, stroking him until he has grown as hard as before. It does not take long.

I'm sitting on the balls of my feet, with my ass up in the air. The head of his cock pushes against me and I can wait no longer.

He fills me completely when I settle down on top of him. His eyes close again immediately and he grabs hold of my hips hard, attempting to keep me in place.

It's been ages since my last time. He stretches me to my limits. So pleasurable, it hurts a little. Or so painful it's actually pleasure.

I don't know which, only that I need more of it.

I wiggle free from his grasp, and play with his belly and sides, before running my fingernails down his chest. My brain fogs up until it's hard to focus on anything other than finding the right rhythm.

He's perfect and he's all mine. I must tell him this after.

As I ride him, slowly at first, his hands twitch, shifting over my sides and grabbing my tits with the eagerness I had expected much earlier on. He looks so high it's incredible to watch and I want to push him further.

"Ohh, this is even better than I'd dreamt," I whisper.

His head is thrown back against the pillow, eyes

closed and brows pulled together. It's the most gorgeous expression I have ever seen. I speed up and lower myself totally onto him.

With my ass bobbing up and down and my face buried in his chest, once more seeking out his nipples, he stiffens up completely. His fingers dig into my back hard, making me cry out in bittersweet pain.

He spasms and groans and keeps me still in a vice-like grip.

"Fuck, I came already. I'm so sorry," he says.

"Don't be sorry, it's not over yet!"

He takes a quick look at me and grabs my neck to draw my face closer. His kisses are hard, rough, and his hands on me focused. He hits all the right spots, except one.

I shift around to straighten my legs downwards and feel him slipping, but he's eager to compensate. He knows just what to do with his fingers, exactly where I need it.

Now it's my turn to be out of control, tugging at him, scratching. Feeling his sexy body underneath me, cushioning me. He keeps kissing me with a previously non-existent certainty and control. I might be still on top, but he's taken complete charge.

While he does that thing of rolling and plucking at my nipple, I continue to rub up to his hand which remains sandwiched between his thigh and me. I can't hold back any longer. I scream with ultimate pleasure coursing through my entire body.

He releases his strong hold on me and instead lets

his hands explore the contours and muscles on my back. I'm relaxing quickly and move onto my side next to him. It's so calming, the slowing rhythm in which his chest rises under my hand with every breath.

One of my legs is still draped over his thigh and my head rests on his shoulder. My whole body is molded to his, unwilling or unable to let go.

All of it was completely worth the wait and has only made me feel more strongly for him.

If there is a heaven on earth, this is it.

* John *

Her hand is still on me, our legs entwined. She's breathing more slowly and at times her index finger twitches ever so slightly.

I've fantasized about finding someone my whole life, even if over time my hopes changed. Obviously when younger I was mostly preoccupied with sex. Not that there's anything wrong with that.

As I got older, I wrote off passion as something beautiful people experience with other beautiful people. Instead I hoped for closeness and companionship.

But with her I feel it all and more.

I caress her shoulder softly, trying not to wake her, and then rest my hand on her arm. She stirs a little and snuggles against me more. My chest feels close to exploding with urges I've never felt before.

I feel responsible for her happiness, her safety.

At the same time, I want to fuck her in every way imaginable, to hear the screams of her pleasure until she's dripping in cum and sweat.

I'm not sure that's normal. She's so much more than her exquisite body, it feels wrong to objectify her. Yet I can't deny she's capable of giving more pleasure than I ever thought I'd experience.

Her hair feels so soft between my fingers.

She's moving a little again, attempting to wiggle her foot between me and the mattress. There's a chill in the air and her previously feverish skin has cooled. It takes a considerable effort, but I manage to retrieve the duvet that had almost fallen off the bed without disturbing her further.

It tickles slightly when she moves her hand over my belly button. My cock twitches, begging for further attention but I don't want to wake her. So close to her hip it's almost touching but not quite.

Being inside her had indeed felt similar to having her mouth on me—both were mind-blowing. Yet it was somehow different as well.

What surprises me the most about her is how she almost worshipped all those parts of me which I try to wish away on a daily basis. That my body, imperfect as it is, could give her so much pleasure.

Sure, she had already said that she's attracted to me, that my weight doesn't bother her and she actually prefers it. It didn't seem like she was lying, but I couldn't convince myself that she truly meant it either.

Until today.

Once again, I can't resist playing with her hair.

"I love you," she mumbles.
Is this a dream?

VIII.

I have to leave his place early, shortly after waking at seven in the morning. For a moment I just have to close my eyes again though; it's a lovely thing, waking up beside him.

I want more of this!

With a quick kiss on the lips, I release myself from his embrace and make a half-hearted effort to put my clothes on. I can feel his eyes on me from the safety of the warm duvet.

No way am I going into work wearing the same clothes as yesterday. There is something to be said for maintaining a professional image, especially after spending the night naked with a co-worker. Even more so when accusing another of sexual harassment.

"I'm going to get changed at home. See you at work?"

"Alright," John says while stretching.

His hair is messy and he is so obviously only half awake. Just adorable. I really have to force myself to leave.

At home, I hurry to get showered and dressed in the most conservative manner my wardrobe allows. The meeting is at nine sharp and I'd better not be late!

***

Gary's office is obviously a lot bigger, airier and better furnished than anything on our floor. In fact it makes the 'crime scene' look like a pathetic little shack.

John reaches at the same time as me, smiling at me for encouragement. It's my turn first and I'm a little nervous. I am to go through the various points directly related to me from John's list and after me, Tracy is up next and then John.

Gary—already seated behind his large desk—waves me closer and gestures at me to take a chair. He covers the phone with his hand and greets me before continuing to speak with whoever is on the other end.

I note the faint line on his ring finger where a wedding band used to be. Gary's desk is strangely devoid of photographs. Unlike Dick's, who had even hung them up on the walls.

I take the few extra minutes I've got to go through the list of talking points once more. When I finish reading it for the fourth time, someone from HR arrives and sits down beside me.

"Great, now that we're all here," Gary begins to speak.

He explains the purpose of the meeting, to record an official complaint against Dick, before asking me to tell my side of the story.

I start with the beginning; the job interview and his inappropriate stares. Then I move on to the drinks machine incident and remark that there had been times where I caught him looking at me weirdly from across the office. Then there was the unpleasantness at the

Christmas party.

Finally, the so-called performance appraisal yesterday morning, my loud protest and the intervention that followed. I make it clear that at no point did I say or do anything aiming to lead him on. I have always said *no*.

"Thank you, we appreciate your cooperation," Gary says after I'm finished. "On behalf of Aspect Technology, I want to extend a deep apology for all you have been through during your short time in the job. It's inexcusable what happened to you."

I nod solemnly.

He looks over at the HR lady, who is furiously scribbling down notes. His expression tells me he's satisfied with the way things are going.

"What will happen now is that we'll hear from other involved parties, before notifying Richard of everything that's happened and getting his side of things. Based on what you've told me, further investigations will be needed. He will of course be suspended throughout, to avoid further incidents. And we ask that you keep the contents of this meeting confidential.

"It is your right, if you like, to see a counsellor to help you deal with this situation. Please make your request with HR at any time," Gary says.

"Thank you," I say.

When I get out of the office, I notice John is talking to someone in the hallway. The blonde with the long legs and perfectly fitting grey shift dress must be Tracy. I'm not surprised Dick went after her too.

She gives me a nod and walks past me into the

office. Her face is tense, I bet she can't wait to be done with it all.

"How did it go?" John asks.

"Fine, I guess, he seemed to believe me," I say.

"Of course, he did." He smiles at me and brushes his fingers past my cheek and jaw line.

It makes me shiver slightly.

"Last night..." His voice trails off when our eyes meet.

"I know," I whisper.

I desperately want to kiss him, feel him close to me. Relive everything. But due to our lack of privacy, all I can do is stare and bite my lip.

"Are you free tonight?" he asks.

"Probably not," I respond as straight-faced as I can manage.

"Oh." The disappointment in his voice is apparent.

"I was hoping I'd have a date." I can no longer maintain my poker face and blow him a kiss.

Hard as it is, I manage to tear myself away from his beautiful eyes and leave him standing there in front of Gary's office. It's time to get to work.

It's weird, returning to work this morning. Everyone knows, sort of. But I'm sure they all have their own ideas about what really went on in Dick's office yesterday.

Most don't give me a second look, except Amanda, who gets up and comes towards me straight away.

"Cath, glad you're here. Can we talk for a minute?" The urgency in her tone puts me on edge.

I nod and we walk towards my desk. She grabs another chair so we can sit together. Luckily my desk is far enough away from the rest, so our chat won't be overheard.

"Yes? What is it?" I ask.

"Well, about yesterday... and everything." She is plucking at her cardigan.

"I just wanted to say, you know. I'm sorry if things were awkward earlier and on Saturday. I didn't know you and John were an item," she continues.

"Well, we weren't until Saturday itself," I mumble.

Her eyes light up and she leans forward, eager for more details, when she catches herself and backs away again.

"Really, wow... Well anyway, I guess I'm sorry. The girls all talk quite meanly about him, it's easy to get caught up in that... I hope we can still be friendly," she says.

I nod.

"He seems nice enough. Though he keeps to himself a lot so it's hard to form a real opinion," she continues.

"He's wonderful," I say.

Amanda looks at me for a while and impatiently shifts around in her chair when it becomes clear I won't be more forthcoming.

"Yesterday... Did Richard try something in there?" she finally asks.

"I'm not really allowed to talk about it. It's an HR matter now," I say.

"I had a little problem with him, before you joined..."

She looks down nervously at her hands.

"I thought you liked him? I thought everyone did," I ask.

"He has a real issue with accepting 'no' for an answer," she says. "As you might have noticed."

"If he was inappropriate with you, it might be worth going to Gary with it. He's been quite helpful," I say. "The more people come forward, the less likely Richard will get the chance to try this sort of thing again."

She wipes the palms of her hands on her skirt and finally looks up again.

"You know what, I will. I didn't really consider coming out about it before, I mean it's not like anything *actually* happened... I worried that it wouldn't be taken seriously and they'd take his word over mine." She smiles nervously.

"Go see Gary upstairs. Why should we have to feel unsafe coming to work every day?"

"Thanks, Cath." Amanda gets up, back to her desk.

Shock sinks in. So, Dick 'The Pervert' Porter, has a history of preying on women that work in this company and nobody has dared to say a word about it until now? I hope Amanda does the right thing.

The morning creeps by without John anywhere in sight. Surely the meetings with Gary can't be taking this long! Every time I look at the time, a sickening fear builds up in my stomach. Has he been suspended as well? Worse still, what if Dick called the police on him?

Lunchtime rolls around and I'm in no mood to go face the interrogation squad. Neither do I want to leave the office, in case John comes back. So, I just sit around at my desk, fiddling with my phone.

I decide to text Jase.

Hey what's up? Boss made a pass at me and John punched him in the face. Happy days.

It doesn't take long for a response to come in.

Jason: "Babe, WTF! Can you talk?"
Me: "Not now, I'm still there. Am fine, really. Meeting's going on, looks like Boss'll be suspended. Don't know what's going to happen to John yet."
Jason: "Call me, ASAP! And tell me everything Xo"

I put the phone on the desk and stare at nothing. Where is John? Why is this taking so long?

It buzzes again and I check. John has confirmed my Facebook friend request. Finally!

I start typing a message when one comes in from him first.

Sorry things are kind of hectic, I'll be free at 3-ish. I've got big news! See you then <3

Puzzled, I keep re-reading the message. Big news? Gary already confirmed to me that Dick would be suspended, but John never doubted that even yesterday, so he must be referring to something else.

At least it sounds like good news rather than bad. My earlier fear has made way for impatience.

After two more hours of shuffling around paperwork and attempting but failing to do much work, finally it's three pm. I can't stop staring at the entrance, and the minutes pass at a snail's pace while I'm bouncing off the walls.

The doors open and I have to really restrain myself to not jump up. Gary enters first, with John behind him. As the doors close slowly behind them, Gary clears his throat and my previously oblivious colleagues look up from their work too.

"If I may have a moment please, I would like to make an announcement," Gary says.

"You may have been aware that there have been issues with Richard lately. I am not at liberty to go into detail, but it transpires that he will be leaving Aspect with immediate effect." Gary looks over to John, who steps forward in that adorable shy manner he adopts when he's being scrutinized.

"I have appointed John as the interim Purchasing Manager. I trust that I can count on everyone's support, after all he has proven himself as a capable and valuable part of this team during the five years he's been with us."

Oh. My. God.

I'm unsure how to react or what to do, simply stunned with my mouth wide open. John has been promoted! He has got to be the only person on earth who ever got away so splendidly with assaulting his boss.

It takes me a minute to gather my thoughts and look

around. Everyone else also appears to be taken by complete surprise, possibly not in a good way.

Gary pats John on the shoulder and says a few words, of encouragement probably, then turns and leaves again. John meanwhile is just staring in my direction. I don't think he took his eyes off me even once while Gary was talking.

He comes over and I immediately get up.

"Oh wow, congratulations!" I sound hysterical.

"Thanks, I can't really believe this has actually happened yet," he says.

"No, I can imagine! Damn."

"Actually, I'm quite nervous, they all hate me I think," he says as he discreetly nods over at Sharon and the rest of the gossip squad.

"They'll get used to it! At least you're not a pervert; that should count for something." I grin. "Seriously though, you're really good at your job. Everyone knows that."

"Thanks." He straightens himself and looks towards Dick's old office. "I guess I'd better get settled in and make myself useful in there."

"Sure. I'm so happy for you though. We should totally celebrate tonight!"

He makes his way to the office and I go back to my seat.

Wow...

It takes me a whole ten minutes to fight the daze that has come over me. Who would've thought? And then an unpleasant realization forms in my mind. If he's now my boss, and we're dating… Ever since the Christmas party, everyone knows about it too.

Shit, I need a new job.

Or at least an internal transfer. I have no idea how to achieve that so suddenly.

Even good news doesn't make life simpler. I sigh, lean back into my chair and turn my thoughts to possible evening plans. Perhaps he'd like to go out, even if the way he was looking at me suggested he'd much rather just stay in.

For the rest of the afternoon, I do my best to be or at least *look* productive. Thanks to his training, I know what I'm supposed to be doing. Time still passes slowly though.

At five sharp, everyone gets ready to leave. While Dick was in charge, a few of the girls would routinely stay late. I can no longer be sure whether they wanted to impress him by doing extra work or stayed back for other reasons.

The thought makes me sick.

But now, at five past, everyone has already left.

I look back at Dick's old office and spot John in the doorway. I wonder how long he's stood there looking at me. After switching off my PC, I gather my things and join him.

He's smiling widely. There's a boyish innocence about him when he smiles.

We move inside the office, which despite the wonky door still affords some privacy. He places his hand on my waist and pulls me close. I rest my face against his chest and close my eyes. Being apart all day was hard, I've come to enjoy our days at the office together so much.

Butterflies, not just in my stomach but everywhere else inside of me too. Then paranoia gets the better of me and I suspiciously eye the door.

"Does Gary know?" I ask.

"Know what?"

"About us, being together?" I say.

"He seemed to be aware, but we didn't discuss it as such," John says. "Would be impossible for him to have missed it after we showed up at the party together."

"I think I should quit." I look up at him; he's no longer smiling and removes his hand from the small of my back.

"Why on earth would you want to do that?"

"Because now you're my boss." I say. "It's inappropriate, especially after everything that happened. It'll be so easy for people to draw the wrong conclusions."

He thinks for a bit and his expression softens.

"I suppose you're right. It all happened so quickly, I hadn't considered that."

"I'll really miss seeing you all day," I say.

"Same here. Let's try if we can think of a better solution."

He takes my face in his hands and leans down, kissing me gently on my lips. Funny, how such a simple gesture can turn my knees to jelly.

"By the way, last night, you were talking in your sleep," he says.

"Was I?"

"Well, technically you just said one thing."

I swallow, hard. Now that he mentions it, I do have a vague recollection of what I might have said. My cheeks start to burn up. It felt like part of a dream. Apparently not.

When I force myself to look back up, he's smiling again. Warmth and tenderness in his eyes.

"I meant it," I whisper.

"I didn't respond then, but..." He takes a deep breath. "I love you too."

PART IV.

I.

"I love you too," John says.

I'm speechless. And if he wasn't still holding on to me, I might have lost my balance.

He loves me.

It would have been so easy for him to ignore what I said. To sweep it under the rug and avoid the topic.

Everything I've done in this relationship so far was wrong. I've been my usual clingy, needy, intrusive and pushy self. Any other guy would have run for the hills.

But not John.

Of course, all of this is happening way too quickly. How can we be sure about this yet, after such a short time? All I know is that it feels right, though. This feeling I have when I'm with him, I know it's what I've always wanted.

He kisses me again and I cling on to him, both arms wrapped tightly around his neck. It's blissful and I forget where we are. All that matters is how his lips fit mine and his arms keep me steady. My heart might just explode with joy.

"You're perfect, you know that," I whisper.

He just smiles and shakes his head. I can't tear my eyes off him; he *is* .

This near-dream state I find myself in doesn't last. There's a knock on the door and we let go of each other immediately and attempt to look casual.

"Yes?" John says.

Gary walks in; by now I'm sure he must know about us. He looks first at him, then at me, but his face doesn't betray his surprise, if there is any.

"Good, you're still here," Gary says, "It has come to my attention that Richard had arranged to attend a show in Munich this week, all the big suppliers will be there. It'll be a great networking opportunity."

"Right." John straightens himself and waits for Gary to continue.

"I appreciate it's short notice, but still. Your flight would leave in the morning. I'll have the booking details sent to you."

"Sure, no problem," John gives me a quick look before facing Gary again.

"Brilliant, you'll be getting an email shortly." Gary's professional façade slips momentarily when a knowing smile forms on his lips. "Carry on."

When he's out the door John turns to me again.

"I hope you don't mind. He didn't give me much of a choice," he says.

"Of course not." I smile even though I hate the idea. "But first, how would you like to celebrate your promotion?"

We decide on a French restaurant in Teddington. I wonder if he suggested it to impress me or if he truly likes fine dining. Since it's still too early to eat, we escape the frosty December weather by heading into the nearest pub.

It's still quiet at barely six pm, and there are plenty of

seats available. John insists on getting the drinks, while I make myself comfortable on a brown leather sofa so big it looks as though it might swallow me whole.

"What would you like?" he asks.

"Cider. Magners or whatever they've got. With ice," I say.

It's a nice place, very cosy and old-fashioned without looking too aged. Every prop, picture and item of furniture is slightly mismatched, yet in keeping with the overall style. As if someone put a lot of thought into making the decor appear random and eclectic.

Even the barman looks like he's from another era, his dress sense reminding me strangely of René from *'Allo 'Allo*, but fit. They have a little chat, John and René's counterpart, suggesting they know each other. The barman gives me a little nod, gets a couple of glasses. John smiles and glances in my direction too before picking up our drinks.

"Here you are," John says, handing me my pint glass and bottle.

"What are you having?" I ask.

"It's a local craft beer, this is the only place that sells it." He sits down next to me and shows me the logo on the pint glass.

I'm not sure why, but I find it charming that he likes obscure beers nobody else has heard of. Seems like the type of thing I would go for, if only I liked beer.

"So, do you come here often?" I wink at John.

He dramatically throws his hands in the air and rolls his eyes.

"Does that line ever work? Honestly?"

We laugh and clink our glasses together.

"Cheers," I say.

"Cheesy pick-up lines aside, I was asking because firstly I have no idea how you like to spend your spare time and secondly because the bartender seems to know you."

"Yeah, I do come in here sometimes, maybe a bit too often lately," he says.

He looks absentminded, sliding his pint back and forth a few times on the table, as the bottom of the glass leaves a wet swish on the well-worn wood.

"I'd been wondering about that. Actually, I've been worried about you for weeks now." It's all I dare say, not wanting to sound like a nag.

"Yeah, I noticed. Obviously, I didn't understand why you'd care before. But there'll be no more of that now. I promise," he says. Thankfully he doesn't look annoyed with me.

That's all I wanted to hear, so I let the topic go. He was going through a phase, and that's that. After all, he was perfectly fine sticking to just a couple of drinks at the Christmas party.

He puts the glass back down on the table after taking a sip, and I follow his example. I scoot closer to him, nudging at his arm. He gets the hint straight away and puts it around me. The subtle smile playing on his lips tells me he's not awkward at all about being obnoxiously in love in public. *Good.*

"I can tell you this much, it's a lot more fun being

here with you," he says.

His phone rings and he takes it out of his pocket to check. The flight and hotel booking for his trip. I bite my tongue and don't let on that the prospect of his absence, however short, saddens me.

I've got to work on my clinginess before I start getting on John's nerves! My abandonment issues, as Jason likes to say.

"Looks like I'll be leaving at an ungodly hour." He shows me the phone; his flight leaves at seven and the airport is a good hour away by car.

When he puts it away again, he looks over at me in that special manner of his. So warm, and there's also a hint of wonder in his eyes.

"When will you be coming back?" I ask.

"Saturday morning."

I sigh and take another sip. The cider is absolutely freezing with the ice in it, a fairly stupid choice of drink in this season now that I think of it. He notices me shiver and pulls me closer against him again. A gesture which never fails to make everything better.

We get chatting about all sorts, movies mostly. It is quickly decided that we're going to do a regular movie date night at the local cinema from now on.

Another plan is made as well. We plan to watch the whole *Lord of the Rings* saga—which of course I have Blu-Ray copies of—one after the other, marathon style. This weekend.

I'm excited already, to share something I love with the person I love even more.

It'll be our way of making up for the three days apart.

Our glasses empty and it's closing in on seven pm. We decide to head to the restaurant for our well-deserved meal.

Another quaint little establishment, the restaurant is possibly even more charming than the pub. They seat us at a little table for two by the window, amongst the dozen or so others that are either already occupied or reserved.

I had no idea such a place existed just minutes away from my place. But then again, I haven't really made an effort to check out the local restaurants.

There is no joy in eating out alone, at least not for me. I crave company to share bites of food, to laugh with and on this occasion, to help choose the wine. Even if foreign food doesn't faze me, I know nothing about wine.

John is in his element, his cheerfulness infectious. He studies the drinks menu and suggests various options to complement our dishes of choice but I let him have the last word. We're sharing a bottle. I wasn't really paying attention to the name, but I gather it's red.

I simply cannot stop looking at him from across the table as he confidently gives the waiter our order. As if he's been waiting a long time for the opportunity to bring someone here.

"This is a lovely place," I remark.

"Only with you in it," he says.

I blush and awkwardly glance away. He seems to

enjoy it.

Under the table, I carefully slip out of my pumps. It's his turn to blush when my foot finds his ankle and calf, softly caressing him inside his trouser leg. I wish we had more privacy. I could think of all sorts of interesting ways to pass the time until our food arrives.

I take a sip of wine, which truly is lovely thanks to his expert choice, and glance at him. He's leaning forward a bit with his chin resting against his hand and just stares. Carefully observing every move I make, he tries not to react to the little smile I can't suppress.

I let my foot travel upwards. His brooding gaze is interrupted when his eyes involuntarily snap shut upon my reaching his knee.

His flight leaves so early and he'll still have to pack and prepare. We might not get any alone time today after dinner. But that does not discourage me; he's made me wait for it before, now it's his turn. We'll have plenty of time to catch up over the weekend.

The waiter arrives with our entrée, scallops for me and foie gras for him. Beautifully arranged as one would expect, the food is perfect in every way. Its arrival has broken the tension between us a little.

"You'll have to tell me how you know so much about wine," I remark, before putting the glass back down on the table.

"Oh, my mum, she likes to think of herself as middle class. She would organise these dinner parties pretty much every month. The right kind of food, perfect presentation, supposedly posh guests and of course expensive wine." He shrugs. "It was all a bit over the top, but I suppose the wine knowledge stuck. So, what are your parents like?"

The way he grew up is very different from my own childhood. I shrug. "They're not really in the picture."

He doesn't say anything. Perhaps he's equally unwilling to ruin the current mood.

I casually dive into my plate again. The perfectly cooked scallop simply melts in my mouth.

"The food here is simply amazing," I say.

"I know."

John smiles and offers me a bite of his starter as well. Both dishes are very impressive and it does not take long before we've cleaned our plates.

Time passes too quickly. Before we know it, the night will be over, and he'll be getting ready for his trip. I hatch a little plan to commemorate the evening, short as it may be.

Before the main course arrives, I make an excuse and visit the facilities. When I appear next to John again, I make sure my return is carefully timed to avoid onlookers. I lean over and discreetly deposit the contents of my hand in his pocket.

"I thought perhaps you'd like to carry a little something of mine with you to Germany," I whisper in his ear, before sitting back down.

He slips his hand into his pocket. His confused expression immediately changes once his fingers brush past the soft lacey texture of my discarded panties. Before he's able to say a word, the waiter arrives with our food.

As expected following the starters, the rest of the meal doesn't disappoint either. My enjoyment is heightened by his stares which have become even more intense now he knows I'm panty-less. Clearly he is having a hard time keeping calm and has given up on small talk completely.

When the waiter returns to ask about dessert or cheese, John cuts him off mid-question and asks for the bill. His impatience makes me smile.

As soon as we leave the place, he pulls me close with his arm around my shoulder until his lips almost touch my earlobe. His breath burns hot against my skin when he starts to speak.

II. JOHN

"It's a risky thing, to keep on pushing me like that," I tell Cath.

"Oh yeah? What am I risking?"

She's taunting me. I like it.

"For one, you might've had to go to bed hungry."

"There's no way I'd be hungry for long once we're in bed," she says.

She's right. My body reacts immediately.

I'm fed up with feeling crippled by doubts and worries until she takes initiative. Not this time. If all her teasing suggests what I think it does, she's eager for me to step up. No more Mr. Shy Guy.

I need to get home and prepare for an early start tomorrow, I know that. She knows it too. But here we are, walking through the cold and empty streets. The occasional broken street light means parts of the way home are plunged in darkness. And she has no panties on. I seize the opportunity upon noticing an empty alley off to the right.

She lets out a surprised shriek when I spin her around into the turn and pin her against a flaky wooden door which looks like it hasn't been opened in decades. When I kiss her, she does not protest. One might think she's been waiting for exactly this.

I press up against her, encouraged by her hands which furiously fight the buttons on my coat and slip inside. She squeezes the flesh over my sides, tugs at me to come nearer and sends me into a frenzy of lust. She wants this as much as I do. Why, I don't know. Does it matter?

When she let her foot travel over my legs, softly caressing me under the table earlier, that's when I started to get hard. Not only has my cock developed a mind of its own now, I've become painfully sensitive to the slightest bit of attention from her. I was done for after her short trip to the ladies' room.

My hands roam her body. I'm a slave to her.

Helplessly enchanted by the curves of her hourglass figure. How her waist dips in just enough for my hand to find a perfect spot to rest above her lush hips. Those eyes that I know to be a mysterious blueish-green but which just look black in this light.

The most beautiful woman I've ever seen. And she's all mine.

I squeeze her thigh through the loosely fitted knee-length skirt. It's not nearly as suggestive as some of the other outfits that I've seen her in, but that doesn't disguise her appeal. I know enough of what's underneath to drive me mad regardless.

She moans in my ear and tilts her hips in my direction. Her hands are warm against my back, taking their time to work through every tense muscle on their way down. Then she grabs my ass, hard. I'm surprised how good it feels.

"Cath, I need you..." I groan.

She lets go on one side and brings her hand forward,

exploring the contours of my aching erection through my trousers. It's almost too much but I'm just about able to fight back the fogginess that threatens to cloud my mind.

"Do you?" she teases. "How much?"

With both hands on the hem of her skirt, she lifts it for me. Although she's worn her tights again, the outlines of her labia are visible underneath the sheer barrier. I hold my breath and touch her. Sure enough, she is so wet the Lycra has a moist patch seeping through which reaches halfway down her thigh.

She tries to pull the tights down but I shake my head. No need. I pinch the fabric between forefinger and thumb and pull. It's surprising how easily it gives way, splitting open right at the crotch.

Looking down at what I've done and then back up at me, she licks her lips and stares at me. Her eyes defiant and fiery. She's daring me to continue.

I slip one finger into her, then another. She writhes against the doorway, panting and moaning already. Upon steadying herself with her hand against my chest, she hitches one leg up to allow me better access. The sight of her drives me almost to despair but I will myself to continue.

Meanwhile she seeks to free my trapped cock but her hands are impatient and shaky. She manages it after a few tries and the cold air stings against my exposed skin.

"If you can reach..."

She's got me by the balls, and gently directs me towards her.

How? My initial worry subsides when she adjusts her angle and positions herself. Legs spread wide across my thighs, hips angled and one hand hanging on to the protruding door frame overhead. She already knows it'll work, I realize. All I need to do is hold her steady and aim.

I plunge into her. She's tight, but also sopping wet. Before I'm able to wonder how best to move, my hips and hers twitch, finding their natural rhythm. A few times it's dangerously close to slipping, but I continue to fuck her against that door, enjoying the soft moans she so desperately fails to suppress.

Every thought in my head is aimed at putting off the inevitable, the release I've been dying for since she gave me that look at the restaurant. The one which screams 'I want you' more than the equivalent words ever could.

I kiss her forehead and nearly forget my purpose, continuing to push her closer to salvation as wayward locks of her hair tickle my face. Her free hand twitches against my back, nails dig in for grip but not finding any. She moans again, words fragmented by numerous hot gasps that hit my neck.

"Ohh... I'm gonna... Harder!" She finishes with clenched teeth.

The hand that was keeping her positioned and steady from the ledge above us slips, and her back hits the door with a pronounced thud. Before I'm able to worry about hurting her she clings to me with both arms locked around my shoulders and continues to grind her hips against my cock.

Her lips are hungry for mine, but pause momentarily as her body goes rigid. My wait is over, which is lucky because it would have been impossible to hold on any longer. I try not to make too much noise as I push into her one last time.

Barely aware, mind-numbing pleasure overpowers my body and mind. Something goes slightly wrong. Whether due to my angle or the sudden limpness in her body, I slip. My cum ends up dribbling down both her thighs.

She straightens herself, finding balance on her own two feet again. Then she looks down at herself and back up at me, one eyebrow raised but unable to disguise the glint of amusement in her eyes.

"Tease me again at your own peril." I chuckle.

She steps out of her shoes one at a time and takes off the ruined tights, scrunching them up and using them to eliminate most of the evidence of what just happened.

"It's not that I'm complaining, but damn. You're quite the animal when you want to be," she says.

Her hair is still dishevelled as she smooths down her skirt and closes her coat up all the way to the top. Beautiful, filthy girl. Her hands move on to me, resting against my chest for a moment. I'm reminded to get myself in order. While I do that, she stands on tiptoe and melts me with a tender kiss.

"You continue to surprise me." She smiles and turns to discard the tights somewhere out of sight.

I could say the same.

It suddenly strikes me that had I observed a scene like this only a week ago, I might have made certain judgements about the people involved. And I would've been very wrong. I love her for showing me such beauty, or no—everything is beautiful because I love her.

We continue on our earlier path home, as if nothing ever happened. Arms wrapped around each other, I'm acutely aware of the frosty air now. She must be freezing.

When I look over, I see her cheeks are a healthy pink and her expression content. She notices my attention and smiles at me again.

I wish I could take her home with me. And then I'd be tempted to smuggle her along on the trip—in my suitcase if I had to. In an ideal world I'd spend every single night with her, loving her in every possible way.

Truthfully, I crave the sex as much as the prospect of knowing she'll be next to me when we sleep, to be the first thing I see upon waking up. And then I'd have a very hard time letting her out of my sight all day.

I've never been this obsessive about anyone, or anything. Is this what love does to people? Or at least that's what it's doing to me, because I very much doubt she's as juvenile and irrational about the whole thing as I am.

By the time we reach her place, my heart feels heavy. I know it's only for a few days, but it somehow seems like an unnaturally long time to be apart.

She reaches up and gives me a peck on the lips.

"Let me know when you've landed safely?" she says.

"Sure," I respond.

She looks at me for a moment.

"What?"

She shakes her head and smiles awkwardly.

"Nothing, never mind," she says.

Then she reaches up again and puts her arms around my neck tightly. Still a bit lost in thoughts, her warm face against me reminds me not to just stand there and do nothing. So, I hug her back and feel just a little bit more torn between having to leave and wanting to stay.

"I'll miss you," she says, "Goodnight."

"Me too," I respond.

She lets go and smiles again before rushing inside. I'm still deciding between staying or going when the click of the door makes that choice for me.

III.

With John away on his trip, my morning at work is slow and a bit bleak. Now that he's obviously no longer working alongside me, Amanda has taken over that role. I suppose it's as good a solution as any.

The amazing events of last night are still on my mind. Never did I think that despite all the teasing and flirting I did, he'd end up *taking me* outside. He did surprise me, in a good way.

And even if I was sad our evening ended when it did, I couldn't help but phone Jase; excited to catch up. Of course, he wanted to hear all about all the work drama as well as the private stuff and it ended up being quite a long phone call.

When I told him John had used the *l-word* already, Jase reacted with apprehension. He warned me not to get sweet-talked into bed and not to get ahead of myself. I had to clear up the order of things. That he'd said it *after* we'd already slept together. And if anything, I had been trying to get *him* into bed rather than the other way around.

Apparently we're both equally crazy according to Jase, who couldn't help but laugh in the end. I'm still smiling recalling the conversation now.

Meanwhile, Amanda tells me she did go to Gary, and told him everything. And she feels much better about coming into work now that Dick (we're both calling him that now) is no longer in charge. I must agree with her; the atmosphere at work is more relaxed now, for most of us.

Sharon is the obvious exception; she looks grumpier than ever. But I've decided she doesn't deserve my attention or concern.

After a while, I get a message from John. He's reached safely, checked into his hotel and now has a busy day ahead of him at the exhibition, but he's thinking of me and will call whenever he's free tonight. This is all the encouragement I needed to do something silly.

My email, titled 'Open when alone' is sent at lunchtime from the staff facilities. Careful not to be recognizable in case it falls into the wrong hands, it's basically a cleavage shot. *Can't wait for Saturday!*

Afterwards, I find myself back at my desk and slightly bored.

"Cath, have you got a moment?" Amanda has appeared out of nowhere and sits next to me. *Wonder where she's been for the past two hours.*

"Sure, what's up?"

"I was wondering if you'd like to hang out tomorrow night, we'll have a few glasses of wine, some dinner. Just a girls' night out, that sort of thing," she says. "It would be nice if we could be friends..." She looks down, fiddling with the hem of her knitted dress.

"Yeah that sounds like fun," I respond.

A grateful smile appears on her lips when she looks back up at me. There appears to be more she wants to talk about, but she remains quiet. Perhaps she's going to wait until after those few glasses of wine before opening up.

Could we be friends? I suppose so, I have nothing against her personally. But what really rubbed me the wrong way was just how she seemingly goes along with anything that happens in the office. She's a bit of a pleaser, careful not to make waves.

But I would welcome a little distraction to keep me from staring at my phone all night. I just know I'm going to waver between texting or calling him, and wondering if I'm being too pushy. And whatever I do, I'll overanalyze it to death.

When the day is almost over, I take a moment to browse the company intranet. John might not be here this week, but I haven't forgotten my concerns about working together now that he's been promoted.

Another department has posted an admin job. It looks interesting. Suitable. I'll have to go through a normal application process and attend an interview, but I'm determined not to ask John or anyone else for any favors. This, I'll manage on my own.

***

My evening is uneventful, until John calls at seven-thirty. My phone rings right in the middle of me heating my dinner.

"Hey," he says.

"Hi, how was your day?"

"Uneventful, until... you know," he answers.

Score.

"I've been thinking about you. A lot," I breathe.

He laughs.

"You're devious, sending me an email like that. I haven't been able to focus all afternoon," he complains.

His tone tells me he didn't mind one bit.

"That was the general idea. You put me in a similar quandary with your antics last night."

I can hear his breathing change on the other end of the line. It's more urgent, shorter.

"Don't tell me you didn't enjoy that." The tone of his voice makes me shiver, or perhaps it's the memory he's conjuring up that does it.

"In that case, don't pretend you didn't like my picture," I tease him back. "Perhaps you should look at it again to remind yourself."

He sighs deeply.

"Well now that you have my undivided attention and you've clearly ignored the warning I gave you last night... How do you suppose we resolve this situation?"

While he speaks, I put my half-heated dinner back in the fridge and get comfortable on the sofa. I'm definitely no longer hungry for food.

"Well, you could start by telling me why you haven't been able to focus..."

"That should be obvious. The subject line of your email had me hiding in the men's room at the convention center..." he says.

"And then?"

"Tragically I only had a few minutes, because I was

on my way to a meeting," he continues. "But seeing your picture nearly made me forget all about that. You look breath-taking, by the way."

"Thank you," I say. "Then?"

"Barely paid attention to the presentation and unfortunately bagged myself some unwanted company for dinner. I've only just made it back to the hotel room now, with fingers itching to dial your number."

I grin at the thought of what else his fingers might be itching for and lean back into the soft cushions of the sofa. I remember only days ago, we made out here, for the very first time.

"What are you wearing?" I ask, fully aware of the cliché.

"Just a suit, white shirt. I've just taken off my tie."

"*Tsk tsk tsk*, as usual, you're overdressed for the occasion. But I can forgive you, because you look super sexy in a suit." With my legs stretched out, I cover most of the length of the sofa.

"Before you take it all off, how about you send me a picture too?" I suggest.

He hesitates.

"But unbutton your shirt first...."

There is rustling on the other end of the line, some form of activity as yet unseen. Luckily it does not take long, because I'm not in a patient mood.

"Alright you should get something shortly." John still sounds a bit hesitant, but sure enough the buzzing against my ear alerts me to a new message.

It's slightly fuzzy and grainy, but there he is on the

display of my phone, shirt open as requested and looking up shyly into the camera. He's clearly out of his comfort zone, but even so, he still looks delish.

"Mm, very nice! You realize you wouldn't be wearing those formals anymore if you were here. I sure am not..."

Looking at the picture again, I can just about make out the typical business hotel surroundings of his room, white sheets, pillowcases and grayish blue fabric headboard behind him. All of it makes for a pretty accurate mental image.

He deserves a look as well, so I quickly take one of me. Revealing ivory satin nightie with lace trim along the top, nipples visibly poking through the fabric and an angle which allows my bare legs to be in full view. The hem slipped up so high up my hip that it's a wardrobe malfunction waiting to happen. *Send.*

I know he has received the picture because I can hear what sounds like a sharp intake of air between his teeth.

"You're so hot," he whispers.

"And what are you going to do about that?" I tease.

"I'm going to have to insist on seeing you the very moment I'm back from this stupid trip," he says.

"Agreed. But for now," I sigh into the phone. "We'll have to make do hearing each other's voices."

"You're killing me, you know that! I never imagined I'd be this frustrated." He sounds quite desperate, so of course I decide to play with him a bit more.

"It probably won't help your level of frustration to

know that I've started to get quite wet while talking to you," I say.

"No, indeed."

"I want you to get comfortable and close your eyes. Touch yourself and imagine I'm the one doing it..." Even before I finish the sentence, his breathing intensifies yet again.

"Only if you do the same..." His voice sounds strained and the rustle of sheets and bedding is audible in the background.

"I've just settled down on the sofa. Imagining your hands skimming over my thighs, reaching almost to the top and then changing direction and heading up and over my hip bone and sides. I love how you touch me. You're so much more patient than I am..." I close my eyes and picture him lighting up his dull, impersonal hotel room.

He is no doubt lying back on the bed by now, hopefully undressed already.

"That's because it would be criminal to rush. You deserve to be treated like the goddess you are," he says.

Such a way with words.

I can barely breathe and let my fingers cup over my breasts which are painfully tense and starved for attention.

"My nipples are so hard they've started to hurt. I want to feel your lips on them..." I moan.

"Something else is hard as well," he responds.

"Would you like me to suck it for you?" I breathe, exploring the wetness between my legs with my finger.

His groan fails to drown out the repetitive rustling in the background.

"Or perhaps you would like to spread my legs and fuck me deeply. You could be on top this time," I say, "I'd like that so much better than anything I can do with my own fingers."

The speed with which he's stroking himself seems to be intensifying. With index and middle finger, I give my clit a few gentle taps before heading further down again and coating myself in my own personal lubricant.

I've never been a great fan of manual stimulation, preferring a vibrator, or better yet, a cock to do most of the work. But the memory of how his light brown eyes burn into me when he wants me—just like last night—has done most of the warm up for me already.

His ragged breaths through the phone are the icing on the cake.

"Tell me everything you'll do to me on Saturday," I say.

He sounds utterly breathless when he responds and his voice doesn't fail to give me shivers. It's so very titillating to be able to hear pleasure in his tone. And the memory of what he looks like when he's this high, oh my...

"The moment I'm back, I'll want to taste you.... your lips, neck... those gorgeous nipples of yours. Will you let me eat you out?"

A loud moan escapes me as my fingers move furiously over my slippery swollen lips and around the protruding tip of my clit. His shallow breaths are a clear indicator that he's close too.

"Of course, I'm yours to do with as you please. Damn I'm about done already!" I bite down on my lip and let my fingers explore my depths, pressing and rubbing faster and faster.

"I wish I could've seen you play with yourself while you were watching me in the shower. To see you hard and ready for me, it's such a turn on," I say.

I'm nearly there, still so frustrated that we're apart tonight. Luckily my imagination is vivid enough to see glimpses of his face flushed with lust and that sexy, lush body of his which seems especially built to fulfil my every desire. I imagine him stroking his whole length while staring me down until I can't resist anymore. I'd take him over the edge with my mouth, aiming for complete loss of control.

"Oh fuck," he grunts.

The raw quality in his voice causes another wave of feverish excitement to descend over me. I press my thighs together, trapping my finger inside me and focus on joining him in his orgasm.

It hits me with such intensity I scream into the phone in a manner that would've made a porn star proud.

And then, neither of us makes much of a sound anymore. We're sated and allow ourselves a moment of quiet to fully enjoy it. Breaths previously competing against each other in short bursts are now slowing in tandem. A post-orgasmic need for closeness overcomes me and I grab a cushion to cuddle with but it's quite a pathetic stand-in.

After a short breather, we start talking and time passes at lightning speed. I tell him about my plan to go out with Amanda tomorrow, to which he responds that he also has plans with a supplier. Or rather, plans were already made with Dick, so now he's automatically included as his replacement. Then he changes the topic.

"Tell me about your family. You said Jason is like a brother to you? But not your *actual* brother, right?" he asks.

I bite my lip. It's an awkward question. I'd much rather hear more about his mum's pretentious dinner parties. Still, I yield and tell him my sad history.

About my mum who couldn't even take care of herself, never mind a child. And how Jason's family provided refuge when I needed it the most. It's been a long time since I thought in depth about those days.

John is sympathetic, caring. He doesn't make me feel inadequate or weird even once.

Before we know it, my phone bleeps into my ear to complain about the battery level and it's bedtime anyway. Had he been here, we might not have talked all this much, instead focussing on physical affection and further exploration. But this long conversation has brought us closer together. In a way it's a good thing he had to go on a trip this week, forcing us to connect in other ways than just sex.

"Goodnight." I yawn into the phone and stretch leisurely.

"Love you," he says.

"Love you too." I hang up with a smile on my face and tightly wrap my arms around the cushion I'm still holding.

IV.

The next day passes much like the previous one. Amanda and I are working well together, but in the afternoon she leaves for a while again.

I decide to spend my alone time writing an application to HR for that admin vacancy I found yesterday. If it works out I'll have one less thing to worry about. It would be nice to at least be able to remain in the same building as John; I had only just started to get used to the place too.

And it is so near to home; only a short bus ride away.

At five to five I start gathering my things, as does Amanda, who has just come back from wherever. I am curious but decide it's none of my business.

"Ready?" she asks.

I nod. We head to a local bar she's picked for a few drinks. Who knows what the rest of the night holds?

It's a fancy place, quite the opposite of the pub John took me to the other night. Flashy. Blue lighting and lots of mirrors. I think I prefer his choice over Amanda's but I'm not about to complain.

Perched on the steel and black leather bar stools, we get settled in and start with fairly uninteresting small talk. Almost at the end of the first glass she brings up what I assumed she wanted to talk about all along.

"It's been a lot better at work without Dick there, hasn't it?" she starts.

I couldn't agree more.

"But what has really bothered me, the talk that's been going on ever since John's promotion," she says.

"Oh?"

"Well, you already knew they're all a bit... well... Sharon hates him especially, she feels that if anyone deserved to take over it was her," Amanda continues.

"She's been telling everyone that you and John set Dick up. Of course, I know that's really not the case."

"And do the others believe this nonsense?" I ask.

Amanda shrugs.

"I don't think so, but you know how they are. Nobody will openly talk back to Sharon."

I sigh and take another sip of wine to fill the silence. Amanda follows my example.

"Did you tell him that I told you about his ex? About the phone call?" she asks finally.

So this is what she's been awkward about! *Now we're getting somewhere.*

"No, just that I'd heard rumors about it," I lie.

She seems relieved.

"I really felt bad for him. Maybe I shouldn't have told you, but then it did explain a lot, didn't it? I wasn't sure if you had taken a liking to him already at that time."

"I did, from the start," I mumble.

She touches my arm and when I look over at her I see she's smiling.

"Cheer up, I think you make a really sweet couple. He's changed so much during this week, it's amazing.

You make him happy."

I smile back at her. She's right, he has changed for the better. He makes me happy too.

Her remarks encourage me to open up more.

"I do wonder, how can he ever fully trust me after what she did to him, you know? And having the entire conversation overheard by the whole damn office... How do you come back from that?" I'm thinking out loud. It must be the alcohol.

"Just be good to him, I'm sure it'll be fine. Have you seen the way he looks at you? Obviously he's not thinking about any of that!" She grins at me.

I can't help but give her a wide grin back. We signal the bartender for refills.

"So, love at first sight then." Amanda runs her fingers down the stem of the full-again wine glass.

I nod and bite my bottom lip.

"When I was offered the job, I saw him through the window of Dick's office. I can't quite put it into words," I say.

"Try anyway," Amanda encourages me.

"I was just... helpless. Knew I had to get close somehow. Those first few days working together were tough. I was just a bundle of nerves and didn't know what to do or say around him." I smile before looking at Amanda again.

"And it doesn't bother you that he's..." She looks away again and takes a sip.

If we're going to have *this* conversation, I'm not about to make it easy on her. "That he's what?"

"You know... I'm sorry, but I'm just going to come out and say it, he's a bit... overweight." Amanda has turned deep red by now.

"No, it doesn't. I don't understand why people make such a big deal about this. I actually like it. Aren't dad bods in nowadays?" My voice sounds more confident than I feel.

It's odd talking about it; only very few people know about my preference and at least one of them—Greg— took it very badly. Then I remind myself that it doesn't matter what *she* thinks.

She sits quietly and looks at me for a while.

"Okay, so hypothetically, if you had the choice between him how he is now and still him but he'd be all fit, underwear model types?" she asks.

"I wouldn't change a thing," I answer without hesitation.

"Wow, that's..." She pauses.

"Weird?" I ask.

"No, I think it's really nice. To be wanted and appreciated for who you are, isn't that what everyone wants? He's a lucky man."

We sit, both lost in our own little worlds, while finishing our second round. I wonder what John is up to, whether he's also sitting somewhere in a bar with work people from the trade show. If he's thinking of me at all.

When our next refill arrives, she turns to me again.

"You know... I think I like Gary."

I pause, the wine glass inches from my lips and look

over. Her eyebrows are raised just slightly while she waits for me to react. She's not joking.

"Oh? He seems nice I guess," I say. "He's single?"

"Recently divorced." She looks away again, a subtle smile playing on her lips.

That makes sense. I remember that he wasn't wearing a wedding ring anymore when I met him in his office.

"I always liked older men. But I never admitted it to anyone before," she says.

"Well obviously I've not thought of him that way. But yeah, I can understand the appeal."

Gary and Amanda, I'm surprised and yet not really. He's not a bad looking guy, even if his grey hair and well defined, sharper features suggest that the gap between them must be at least fifteen years. And he does exude that certain—power is the wrong word—authority? That sort of thing can be very tempting.

"Do you know how he feels about you?" I ask.

She smiles again.

"He made the first move actually. Called me into his office yesterday and asked me out." Her cheeks are flushed again.

So here we are, three drinks and several intimate confessions into the evening. Perhaps we *can* be friends. There's more to Amanda than meets the eye. Even if she remains a bit of a people pleaser.

Rather than complicate matters in our slightly tipsy condition, we opt to eat food next door. Italian.

Afterwards, we promise to do this again sometime

soon. It's nice to have someone to confide in who's actually physically here. I love Jason and we've remained close even after he moved away. Still, I've been missing that special connection you can only get when the other person is physically around.

I reach home at a little after eleven and simply have to mess with my phone before going to bed.

'*Thinking of you... Goodnight.*'

I wait for five minutes or so. No response.

V.

TGIF! I'm counting the hours, minutes, seconds. Once today passes, it won't be long until John gets back. We haven't strictly agreed on a time to meet yet, I'm going to let him take the initiative.

In any case his flight isn't going to arrive until ten am tomorrow.

Unlike other days, today Amanda disappears before lunch rather than after. When she gets back to her desk around eleven, her hair is not strictly messy but oh so subtly out of place. Now that I have a pretty good idea what she's up to, her guilty smile makes me chuckle.

The little …!

Before I get the chance to say anything to her, my direct line rings. HR. They've received my application and are phoning to arrange an interview with the Sales department head.

I never expected to hear back so soon. Either they want to fill that opening very urgently, or perhaps they're trying to pacify me after the nasty business with Dick.

One thing that's bound to come up during the interview is my reason for wanting a transfer so soon. And since Gary instructed me not to say anything about what's really going on, I don't have much time to think about a plausible answer.

The interview is scheduled for one-thirty, so I spend

lunch at my desk, preparing and drinking some tea to calm my nerves.

With ten minutes to spare, I make my way to the correct floor and wait. My arrival doesn't go unnoticed; before I get the chance to find a seat somewhere, a door behind me clicks open and I hear footsteps coming in my direction. I turn to find a well-dressed man in his mid-thirties.

"Hi, you must be Catherine. Mark Lloyd." He smiles at me as we shake hands.

"Nice to meet you. Sorry, I hope you don't mind I came a little early," I say.

"No problem, I'm free anyway. We can get started now if it's all the same to you?"

I nod in agreement and Mark leads me into his office. As we sit down opposite the desk, I can't help but notice some things about him. Firstly, the stylish suit which fits him like a glove and manages to subtly demonstrate that he must visit a gym regularly. And his hands, perfectly manicured, which attempt to locate my CV and application from the stack of papers on his desk.

When he looks up and smiles again, a row of straight, white teeth greets me. It occurs to me that he doesn't look like he belongs. Everything about him is too perfect; like we're in a movie and he's an actor playing a role.

Regardless, he seems harmless. Not a hint of that creepiness Dick exuded from day one.

"Just a second, it's here somewhere," he says, "Ah

yes."

He places the documents in front of him and skims through them.

"So, you've applied for the sales admin role..."

"Indeed," I respond.

"Are you not happy where you are now, in the purchasing team? I see you've only joined recently."

"Actually, before I started here, I had worked in other strictly admin jobs before and to be honest, within Purchasing, I'm struggling a bit with the technical aspects; the products and technology we're dealing with. It's a lot to learn from scratch."

This was the best reason I could come up with. A lot more professional than 'the manager tried to molest me and now I'm sleeping with his replacement'.

"That's understandable. I also see here you've also worked as a PA before..." Mark points at my CV.

I take my time to explain what that job entailed and answer his questions. It's becoming more and more obvious that the focus of this interview has shifted away from the sales admin job completely. Mark explains that his assistant has recently moved on and he hasn't yet had the chance to advertise that vacancy.

The entire interview is quite pleasant and conversation flows smoothly. He has a way of making me feel at ease; clearly, he's good at his job. A skilled salesman and negotiator. Even though I know I'm being 'handled', it doesn't feel sleazy.

As the meeting comes to an end, I think I have a good chance. What he's looking for seems to match my experience exactly and I did enjoy the work in my previous job. It's all about who you're working for that matters.

Had Dick insinuated that he wanted me to become his PA during my first interview here, I would've run for the hills.

We shake hands again and he tells me he will be in touch. *Hopefully.*

When I get back to my desk Amanda hurries over.

"Someone's been looking for you..." She points at John's office where the lights are on and the door open. My heart skips a whole lot of beats.

I put my stuff on my desk before rushing off. With a token knock on the door, I step into his office.

"Hey, you're back early!" I say.

John looks up from his computer. I can't quite read him; his eyes are vacant.

"Yeah I got here at around two. Where have you been?"

I close the door behind me and approach his desk. He does not get up. Why is he being so weird?

"I found an opening on the intranet in the Sales department and they called me for an interview already." I wait by his desk, not sure whether to keep standing or sit down as well.

"Yeah, Sharon mentioned you were seeing Mark on the third floor."

"That's right, he was interviewing me."

So, Sharon told John that I was with Mark. Looking at his odd behavior I have to conclude that she didn't make it sound like I was there for work reasons. *The bitch.*

John is looking at his computer again, face tense.

"Good looking guy," he remarks.

"Meh."

Ironic that the morning after worrying out loud in front of Amanda that John might have developed some trust issues somewhere along the line, I get another taste of the same. First with Jason, and now Mark Lloyd. He's jealous again.

"What exactly did Sharon tell you?" I take a few steps forward and lean against the desk right next to where he's sitting. My heart is pounding in my throat and I'm halfway between panicking and getting pissed off.

"He has a reputation, you know," John says.

"I was there for a job interview," I respond. "It's probably logged in the system somewhere if you want to check. Sharon has a reputation as well."

When I put my hand on his shoulder, he flinches slightly. It hurts, all I want is for him to believe in me, in us.

"John, I'm not interested in Mark or any other guy. All I'm trying to do is to get a transfer so we can at least keep working in the same building together."

He shakes his head but doesn't respond.

"Sharon is a spiteful bitch who wants your job. Of course she's going to mess with your head."

She is so going to hear about this! The last thing I need is for her to stick her nose where it doesn't belong.

When he looks up again, it seems like I'm finally getting through to him. He looks sad, or scared, probably both. It's infuriating that he seems to have a tendency to jump to conclusions with regards to other men. But I know it's not his fault really, after everything he's been through.

I'd better swallow my pride and not make things worse.

"Please get up," I say.

He hesitates but finally does as asked and I hug him tightly.

"I've missed you. Silly, I know, in just two days, but I can't help it."

His arms close around me and he seems to relax, as do I. His touch still has that magic, making me feel calm and safe, no matter how crazy things get.

"So sorry," he whispers.

"It's okay."

"I've missed you too. Wouldn't know what I'd do if you left. It drives me crazy to think that one day you might realize that I'm all wrong for you," he says.

"Shh, that's not going to happen," I say.

"I don't think I could stand to lose you."

Neither could I.

"You won't. I love you. You're the first thing on my mind, no matter what I do or who I meet with." I close my eyes and rest my head against his chest, listening to his heartbeat.

"I try not to... but this is the second time I've doubted you." He sighs.

"It'll be okay."

I reach up, around his neck and kiss him. He responds like a starved man finding his first meal in days. His arms surround me tightly and his forehead rests against mine while he says sorry again.

It's difficult now, but I will earn his trust somehow. This is not my fault or his. He's been let down horribly in the past and it's going to take time to get over that. I just hope he keeps letting me back in when he shuts down.

"So how was the trade show?" I ask after what feels like ages.

"Useless, that's why I changed my return flight. I'm convinced Richard arranged it all just to get a free trip out of it."

I slip my arms around his waist and hide my face in his chest. I've missed this, his scent, the warmth of his body against mine. Everything is starting to feel right again.

"I want you to know I've never cheated on anyone and I'm not about to start now," I say, "I'd never hurt you."

He just stands still, his hands resting on my shoulder and on the small of my back.

"You're... everything," he whispers.

I look up and smile at him. His eyes have come alive again after seeming so blank earlier.

"Your place or mine tonight?" I ask, "I'd very much would like to fall asleep with you, and wake up next to you, and everything else."

He smiles too and traces his finger over my jaw, down until my chin.

"I should unpack my stuff..." he says.

"Then how about, I pick up some fresh clothes from home and meet you at yours after?"

He nods in agreement and I let go of him. Time to get back to work, hopefully the rest of the day will pass quickly.

When I get back to my computer, I see a new email from Mark. My gut feeling about the interview was right, he writes he's offering me the PA position. I can start on Monday, provided he sorts out the logistics of the move with HR.

I'm very excited and a bit relieved. Hopefully John will be cool with the idea now that everything has been cleared up.

John leaves a little early, while I wait until five exactly before heading to the lift.

Sharon is already inside when I join her, and I'm met by her hostile stare. The earlier conversation with John is still fresh in my memory, as well as her involvement in the whole situation.

"Sharon, I know you seem to have some kind of problem with me."

She raises her left eyebrow when she turns to look at me, her expression no friendlier than before.

"Catherine, I have no issues at all with you personally. If you want to entrap your boss and then proceed to sleep with the next in line, that's entirely your business. But it does set the wrong tone around the office."

I glare at her and she responds in kind.

How dare she?

"Richard was a filthy pervert and I'm not the only one he tried to victimize. If you can't deal with reality, that's not my fault," I hiss at her.

She continues to stare back at me defiantly.

"And for the record, John and I were an item before his promotion. Neither of us could guess it was going to turn out this way. It doesn't matter now anyway, because I'm transferring out. If you're so concerned about setting the wrong tone around the office, you ought to look at your own behaviour!"

She turns and faces the door, no change in her expression, save the glaze that has washed over her eye. Is she crying now?

Oh, what do I care? She's still a bitch and I'm furious. Someone had to tell her the truth.

The door opens and we both waste no time getting out of the confined space and into the fresh, icy outdoors, only to stomp off in opposing directions.

At home I quickly gather some items of clothing, toothbrush and other essentials and stuff them into a backpack together with the *Lord of the Rings* Blu-Ray discs; we'd made a plan after all. Plenty of food in the fridge, which is also going into the bag to save on cooking time later.

Before leaving, I quickly change into some jeans. At least I won't be freezing my butt off during the walk over to his place. Only when I am nearly out the door, do I notice an envelope waiting on my doormat. It's probably a bill, or something. I decide to leave it in the kitchenette, unopened.

After battling the freezing conditions on the way, I end up at his door, wind-blown and numb. He opens up and takes my things upon letting me inside. I feel like I'm at home away from home, my earlier anger at Sharon all but forgotten.

"Hi..."

"You look half frozen," he remarks, while brushing a few locks of frizzy and damp hair behind my ear.

This simple gesture makes me feel warm inside, even

if the tip of my nose is only just starting to thaw. I proceed to take off my gloves and muffler, and then slipping my heavy coat off my shoulders.

His place is warm, as I remember it. And that scent, his scent. He's wearing the same black hoodie again. I love him as much in casuals as I do fully suited and booted. Though casuals somehow look more... cuddly.

He observes my every move as I take the food containers out of my bag and carry them into the kitchen.

"Are you hungry?" I ask, looking back to find him appreciating my well-fitting jeans from behind.

"Starving," he says.

Of course he is. Facing the counter once more, I smile to myself while heating the rice and chicken curry I brought. Meanwhile he gathers plates and cutlery.

It turns out that actually we're both famished and we finish our meal in record time. Attentive as always, he makes it a point to comment on how lovely everything is.

By seven we're on the sofa together, finding something to watch on TV. Like a normal couple, just comfortable together without the need for pretence or forced conversation. Like we inherently understand that the occasional silence isn't awkward, but content.

"Oh, I forgot to tell you," I start, "I got the job, I'll start next week once the paperwork is all done."

John pulls me against him and kisses the side of my head.

"Congratulations! I'm really sorry about earlier..."

"Never mind. If the whole thing with Dick taught me anything, it's to be more careful about who to work for. First impressions are good. *Safe.* "

"Glad to hear it." He adjusts himself to get more comfortable and I wrap my arm around him.

Looks like he's no longer worried about Mark, which is just as well. He has no reason to be. I can't even imagine looking at another man that way.

He picks up the remote to change the channel, but I've lost interest. Observing him instead, I note a slight stubble showing after presumably not getting the chance to shave this morning. I like the look.

He frowns and smacks the back of the remote which apparently isn't working quite how it should. Not sure why but it amuses me, so I continue to watch him.

It takes him quite some time, before he realizes that I've been staring.

"What?" He raises his eyebrows and smiles in a wonderfully disarming fashion.

"Just enjoying the view."

"Uh-huh. Sure."

I want to kiss him, to show him how important he is to me and that's the only way I know how. He seems to want the same, because he switches the TV off and takes my hands. Pulling me towards him as he leans back, he treats me to a tight embrace and a gentle kiss on my forehead.

The next kiss, on the tip of my nose makes me chuckle. He can be so sweet. I nuzzle against the side of his face, and enjoy the tickle left on my skin by the onset of his beard.

His hands find my ass, while my lips seek out his. It's unusual, how a kiss can set me alight like this. With hardly any effort or warning, I'm flushed and breathless. I want him with every fiber in my body.

His eyes sparkle, he's equally excited.

I interrupt him mid-kiss and get up. It's time to carry out certain plans I've thought up while packing. He looks surprised and attempts to follow me but I gesture at him to stay put.

"I need you to give me five minutes before coming into the bedroom."

He nods, the earlier glint in his eyes reappearing straight away.

"And there's something else I need you to do for me."

"Anything," he says.

His baritone voice washes over me, making me giddy, but I try not to let on.

"Before you open the door, be undressed."

He opens his lips but I interrupt him yet again before he gets the chance to speak.

"Completely."

With that carefully articulated word, I leave him and rush into the bedroom. I may have packed in a hurry, but I still added a little something interesting from my underwear drawer. Something that is better appreciated with company and hence hasn't been of use to me in ages.

It's a bit tricky, putting on the corset and tightening

it by myself but I manage somehow. The look is quickly completed with a matching wine red and black thong and black, lace-topped stockings.

I take a moment to check myself in the mirror. The under-bust cincher perfectly accentuates what I believe to be my best feature; a slim waist with ample curves both above and below. The stockings help to make my hips look wider, in a good way.

Hair should definitely be left down. And the last finishing touch required is a quick dab of red lip gloss. Candles would have been nice, if a bit over the top. For now we'll have to make do with the indirect light of the bedside lamp bouncing off the ceiling.

Guess I'm probably over thinking this. He would have been happy enough to find me naked.

I climb onto the bed and lean against a couple of pillows to wait for him for what turns out to be not very long at all. My heart starts to pound when I hear footsteps outside. Hopefully he'll like me all dolled up, but then again, why wouldn't he?

He knocks once and after I call for him to enter, the door opens. His reluctance, demonstrated by how slight the crack of the door is, both endears and teases. I can't wait to admire him as I expect he will admire me.

Leaning up onto my elbows, I am making use of how the slightest angling of my head causes locks of my hair to cascade off my chest to reveal my perky breasts. The corset really does make them look bigger, even if they don't need the help.

This spectacle isn't lost on him either as his lingering

gaze reveals.

"Come closer."

He pushes the door open further and I'm treated to a much better view of him. I watch him breathe deeply while he lets his eyes wander over my outfit, or perhaps more accurately the bits not left to the imagination. I shift my legs to the side, allowing me to sit upright in a fairly awkward and constricted manner.

Tied in tightly or not, the corset doesn't bother me, it actually makes me feel so very sexy. I love the way it keeps my posture artificially straightened and my tummy pushed in. I've always liked a bit of pressure there.

He takes a few steps towards me. His body language betrays how uncomfortable he is, but the longer he looks at me, the more changes I see in him.

"You look spectacular," he says. "I could keep looking at you for hours."

"As could I." I reach out for him as soon as his hand comes within reach.

"Okay, admittedly I'd have a tough time just *looking* without touching."

He's growing visibly harder and I feel my own breaths turn erratic, making me faint. I run my fingers over his before tugging at them gently.

"I want you," I breathe.

He gives me a look like he's just about ready to devour me and I fall back into the pillows again. His erection is blatantly obvious as he gets onto his knees beside me. I can't keep my hands off, not off his cock nor the rest of his body.

"I love this..." I say while exploring him with my fingertips, slowly. Savoring each moment.

The curve of his belly which I know to feel exquisite against me and his thighs with their light covering of straight brown hair, which only grows denser just at the knee and below.

"And this..." I trace the few visible veins on his cock with my fingertip and watch how his expressions change under my touch. Tension fades, he shuts his eyes and takes a deep breath.

"Wouldn't change a single thing about you."

His eyelids snap open again revealing pure, animal lust. But instead of giving him quick release, I continue to tease, alternating between fingertips and nails. Scraping and tickling, slowly yet deliberately.

VII. JOHN

She's doing it again, teasing me. Coaxing my wild side out of me until I revert to instinct. And she's damn good at it too.

Spectacular is one word for the image in front of me. Every other term I can think of is too crude to say out loud.

She watches me intently, no doubt taking in every breath, every uncontrollable shiver and twitch and sigh caused by her soft caresses. The tension inside me builds to near unbearable levels and on the one hand I want to give in, but at the same time I'm enjoying her sweet torture.

On her back, she spreads her thighs ever so slightly. Almost as if she didn't mean for me to notice, still it takes my breath away. Her gaze betrays her intentions, it's all part of the game.

Following her example, I try to turn the situation around. Running my fingers up and down her inner thighs until a little moan escapes her. She adjusts herself a bit in an attempt to guide my fingers upwards.

I have other ideas, though. Bending down, I gently blow on her nipples but take care not to let my lips touch. Goose bumps appear.

Her hair is fanned out over the pillows and her lips slightly parted. Red and shiny, I like that. And the outfit... It looks like it was custom made just for her.

Her beauty makes me want to scream. A lot of things come to mind, but mostly that same old question: 'Why me?' Will I ever get used to this? I probably shouldn't, because I don't want to lose sight of how special every moment with her is.

Short breaths cause her chest to rise and fall in rapid succession. I get down on all fours above her, my knees between her widely spread thighs. She cranes her neck upwards, nibbling on my bottom lip. It's a competition, she wants me to take her, yet I want her to say the words first.

We'll both win either way.

Her fingers curl up, nails scratching past my sides. Ticklish but oh so good; I forget to breathe and focus on the persistent throbbing down below. When I open my eyes again, I see her looking down, admiring me as I hover just far enough above her. I should feel awkward about the unflattering angle. Ordinarily I would have, if she didn't look so damn pleased.

How alien it feels, being the object of someone's desire.

She runs her fingers through my chest hair and downwards. This time she's the one holding her breath and a strange sensation overcomes me. Pride, yes that's what this is.

I know what I must do.

When her hand travels further south and closes around my cock I've had enough. I give in. She's in charge.

I straighten myself and give her thighs a firm

squeeze. The lace of the stockings feels rough to the touch, in stark contrast with the silkiness of her skin just above. When I start pulling down her panties, she flashes her perfect teeth at me with a smile. She knows she's won.

Immaculately shaved like I remember.

I let my fingers explore her. Hot and soaking wet. They say you should take your time with foreplay. Fuck that.

She moans and arches up; this tells me that she also doesn't want any more delays. Just as well, because the last shred of my self-control has vanished.

I lower myself while she spreads and guides me. *Is that it?* She nods and I push into her, filling her. Both hands are on my arms now, moving upwards towards my shoulders and pulling me down. She moans in my ear as I try to adjust myself and rest on my elbows.

Any concerns that I might be making her uncomfortable are quickly forgotten when she raises her hips to meet me. Fingers dig into me, keeping me in place. Overcome by a haze of lust, I start to find my rhythm. Her small body underneath me wriggles and moves with me with a surprising strength considering I must be weighing her down.

She moans with every stroke, her hands on my ass encourage me to be rougher.

"Oh God yes! This feels so good..."

Her voice makes me shiver, or perhaps it's the words she speaks which do it. I lean to one side, allowing my other arm to reach up and grab a fistful of hair. Her eyes open wide, initial surprise fades and is replaced by defiance. She lifts her head, tugging against my hold on her hair to find my lips.

We fuse together at both ends, kissing and fucking. Licking, biting and scratching—the latter is mainly her. Just when I start to feel tired, all her muscles seem to clench together, spurring us back into movement. Her moans become progressively louder, rejuvenating me.

I'm about ready to explode, watching her face, so beautiful. Little beads of sweat have formed on her forehead, causing her hair to get damp. She screams and digs her fingers into my ass cheeks, drawing me into her as deeply as possible. I find a final burst of energy and plough into her, hard.

Although her grip on me softens, and her moans quieten down, the aftershocks of her release are still evident on her face. *I did this.* I made her cum again with no direction or guidance needed.

Who would've thought?

Before I know it, I'm turning rigid, quivering and twitching all at once. I see a glimpse of her satisfied smile before my eyes shut. Her lips are on me, as are her hands while she rhythmically grinds up against me. I'm helplessly frozen, drowning in pleasure and super-aware of my cock pulsating, filling her with my seed.

It still blows my mind that she wants this as much as I do.

Not sure how long after, because time seems to have stood still, I try to lift myself but she's still clinging to me.

"Don't go," she whispers.

You always hear about how women love to cuddle after, but most men don't. Guess I'm not most men.

She looks at me with big pleading eyes and I realize this is where I'm meant to be for now. In and on her, tasting her sweet lips a bit longer and enjoying her hands gently massaging my back. We're both a bit sticky, but that's fine; we are one.

I feel myself relaxing uncontrollably and rest my head on her chest for a change. It's quite lovely, no wonder she likes to do this to me. Her hands travel upwards, fingers running through my hair.

"Cath, mind if I ask you something?"

"Sure, go ahead," she responds.

"Is it always like this, so intense? Being together; sex."

She continues to stroke my hair as she thinks.

"Not in my experience... Sure it's exciting being with someone when everything's new, but this, us, goes way beyond that." I can hear her heartbeat speed up underneath my ear. Am I making her nervous?

"Well it does for me anyway," she adds.

I have to agree. This certainly blows away any expectations I might have had. Every adolescent wet dream fades in comparison.

She tries to stir and I give her some room by rolling onto my back. Suddenly overcome with fatigue, I feel neither the will nor the need to cover up. She does get up for a short while though, only to return naked and equally willing to just relax.

Gladly, I pull her close again, resting my hand comfortably between her breasts and enjoying the cool, smooth skin of her back pressed up against me. I wouldn't mind falling asleep like this every night for the rest of my life.

I ask about her night out with Amanda, but start drifting off as she continues to answer.

VIII.

When I get up, John is still sleeping. He looks adorable, messy hair, face cuddled into the plush pillow and I don't have the heart to disturb him. I decide instead that I should go out and pick up some milk for our morning tea.

His bag is on the table. A large conference pad is visible through the half-open zip. I'd better leave a note in case he wakes up.

I take out the pad and flip through pages of text, densely written, trying to find the first blank page. But these are not regular notes, it's more like an essay and a very long one too. Seeing my name scribbled multiple times throughout the text sparks my curiosity.

I flip back to the beginning.

'6th December

Dear Cath,

Before I left for this trip, I didn't think it was possible how much I would miss you. I could see it in your face on Tuesday night that you didn't want me to go either, even if you didn't say it.

I'm sorry if none of this makes a lot of sense, I might be a bit tipsy. I tried my best not to overdo it because I know you worry. Although, it seems that I did, I'm not quite sure how many I've had. That's never a good sign, is it?

I'm at the hotel now, can't get to sleep. I miss you, Cath. And

I wish you were here, because I need to tell you something.

On the plane over here, I closed my eyes and all I could think about was you, I imagined you were sitting next to me. At the trade show, I imagined you'd be here in my hotel room, waiting for me. But of course that was all just pretend. I do hope you're waiting for me back home.

I've done something terrible, I'm not sure how you'll react. And I certainly don't know how to even tell you. These people— you may have emailed with a bunch of them—the guys from MicroSemi, they were of course expecting to meet up with Richard instead of me. They had this trip fully planned out accordingly, I think they got on well with him. I don't quite fit in. They like a drink, food (so far so good) and women.

I wasn't sure what to expect when they insisted on taking me out. After a few encouraging pats on the back and statements such as "Go on, you're our customer. We'll take good care of you..."— we left the show around five and shared a cab into town. Our first stop was some flash looking bar.

It wasn't clear what they were up to at first. We stayed there for hours, sharing business gossip. Who had left which company and joined where. Competitors' quality issues and other fuck-ups; the usual industry trash talk. I had two drinks before switching to soda. The last thing I need is to make an ass of myself on my first business trip.

At around nine-thirty or ten, one of them—Jules—started to get impatient. He mashes up his French and English when he's drunk, I could barely understand a word of what he was saying. Anyway, so he's arguing with the others, I gather he wants to leave the bar. As I said, I couldn't quite understand him. We get up and leave for the next place.

A nightclub.

Very awkward, I thought. A bunch of us suits, in town only for the electronics show, in a club filled with what looked like teenagers. I felt odd and out of place the second we walked in. Strangely, while the other guys were all around forty, it didn't discourage them one bit. They immediately started to mingle, spend on drinks and generally act obnoxious.

A lot of the young girls didn't seem to mind, in fact they happily accepted the attention and free booze. It seemingly took a matter of minutes for them all to be paired up.

That's when the problems started.

I managed to find myself a seat because honestly, I wasn't interested in joining them on the dance floor. But another one of the guys noticed me and kept insisting I shouldn't be such a bore. I tried explaining that this isn't my scene, but it made no difference. The drinks kept coming (though I had switched to coke for most of the rounds) and things got a bit crazy. Two of our group disappeared with some girls and when they came back it seemed like they were on something other than just alcohol.

The club was starting to get quieter, no idea what time it was and someone decided we should move on yet again. I tried to slip away but the other guy again intercepted me and questioned me about why I'm acting like a pussy and told me to just chill out.

He went on and on about how we're just a bunch of guys enjoying themselves and it's 'only a fucking night out'; about how 'we don't meddle in each other's business' (ironic, since he was meddling in my plans to just go back to the hotel). He finished by pointing at all of them saying, 'we've all got wives at home, but that doesn't mean we should deprive ourselves of the occasional bit of fun'.

All I wanted was to just get rid of him so I explained, told him about you. I told him I didn't want this supposed fun. It was like talking to a wall. He just laughed and said: 'Grow a pair, man! What our women don't know can't hurt them.' That sort of bull.

Long story short, I couldn't get rid of him and he was starting to get extremely agitated. I didn't want my first face-to-face with these people to go south so I agreed to stay for one last round and that would be that.

We ended up in another place, a strip club. I fear that's when things got totally out of hand. As I said; I don't remember how many drinks I had, but looking back that seems strange, because I kept ordering soda or coke. At one point, everything turned into a blurry haze. I don't recall everything that happened really. Next I know that we ended up in a private booth with a few dancers somehow. It was bizarre. Wrong.

The girl dancing in front of me couldn't have been much older than eighteen. Way too young. I'm not sure what exactly happened next, it all seemed to merge into a dream.

I was thinking of you. I know I observed you in the shower and it was so wrong but at the same time I couldn't look away. You had captivated me completely in that moment. I thought back to the alley on our way home on Tuesday, how tempting you looked. How you made me feel on top of the world. I opened my eyes and there was the same dancer, rubbing up against me. One of the other guys handed her a banknote. I tried to get away, but I couldn't move and then it went all fuzzy again.

God, I don't know how to explain any of it; I don't think I've ever lost control to that extent. One moment I was reliving those beautiful memories with you. The next she has her hands on me. I wanted it to be you. I'm so sorry, Cath. It was supposed to be you. But something felt off, it was rushed and awkward and I opened my eyes and there she was. I couldn't look at her. Panicked, I pushed her away and got up. The others were too preoccupied to notice and she just stared at me blankly like she didn't really care either way.

So, I zipped up my trousers and ran. I hailed a cab outside to get back to the hotel.

You sent a text; I didn't see it until back in my room. You wished me goodnight. That was three hours ago. It's too late to phone you back now but I need to feel close to you somehow, I suppose that's why I'm writing this. I've changed my flight to tomorrow mid-morning and I'm not sure how to face you when I get back.

Yesterday everything seemed so simple, your photo, our talk at night. Everything was perfect. I keep looking at you, at your face. You loved me then, but will you still love me now?

I don't know what to do. I feel like I've fucked up so badly and thrown everything we have away. You have every right to be angry, I'm so very angry at myself right now too. Every time I look at your picture on my phone I wonder, when I tell you about what happened, will I be able to explain? Will you want to hear the explanation, even? Or will you—rightly so—feel betrayed and want nothing to do with me anymore? Maybe this photo is going to be my last reminder of a time when you didn't hate me yet.

That's why I'm writing it down, this is how I'm going to tell you. And I hope you'll read it until the end. Having stared at your picture for about half an hour now, I'm crying because I may have lost you. I hope you're still reading, because I need to tell you truthfully; I didn't want this to go so wrong.

You're the best thing that's ever happened to me. If you leave, I'll have nothing.

I know I don't deserve you, but know that I need you nonetheless. Punish me if it helps, just don't go.

I'm so very sorry. You're everything to me and I love you so much it hurts.'

I feel like I've been punched in the gut, trampled on even. My eyes are starting to well up but rather than express my hurt, I'm frozen and in shock.

How could he keep this from me? Throughout everything that's happened so far, I've come to develop certain expectations. He's been honest, dependable, or at least I thought he had been so far. Sure, he acted weird about Mark yesterday. Was his distrust towards Mark just disguised guilt over to his own behavior?

Instead of letting myself get annoyed at having to be on the defensive yet again, I had tried to manage the situation then. I explained myself, when I didn't really have to. Afterwards, things seemed normal again.

How could he hide something so big and yet convincingly pretend we're fine? Maybe he's not the man I thought he was. Not trustworthy at all but actually rather manipulative.

I can understand why he would shy away from telling me about this, worried about how I might react. But surely I would've noticed something off about him? Instead he was just how he's always been. I feel tricked. Betrayed.

As I read through the last page again, the initial

shock wears off and is replaced by cold detachment. All of this is too far-fetched, too surreal. I can't deal with it right now. I'm seven years old again, back in my shell. It's time to take care of *me*.

Finding a pen within the same pocket of the bag, I take a deep breath, attempting to focus. I need to think.

More than anything, I need to get out of here quickly and without any complications.

'If only you'd been honest and told me when you had the chance.'

Taking care not to make any noise, I sneak into the bedroom and leave the pad on the pillow next to him. After that I gather up a few crucial items of clothing, my bag, and leave. I can't even bear to look at his face right now or I might lose myself.

I might have given him my heart, but he's not getting my self-respect as well.

My walk home through the rain is suitably depressing. By the time I get home I'm frozen and numb all over, not just on the inside. I can't think of what else to do so I draw myself a bath and curl up in the tub, finally giving in to the sense of loss I should probably have felt earlier.

I don't notice how much time passes while I continue to cry. The water turns cold, so I top it up twice. The phone rings, but I'm in no mood to talk to anyone right now so I don't even check.

Another while later it rings again and I grab it to switch off the sound.

It's Jason.

Blinking some of the tears away, I figure I might as well answer.

"Hi," I say.

"Hey, darling, just wondering what you're up to." Jason's tone tries but doesn't quite manage to cheer me up at all.

"Nothing."

"Your voice sounds really weird, where are you?" he asks.

"In the bath."

"Okay, Cath, I love you—you know I do. But I didn't need the mental image of you, naked, in the tub!" Sadly his joke misses its desired effect completely.

I close my eyes and let out a choked sob.

"Sweetheart, what's wrong?"

I take a deep breath but instead of starting to explain what happened, I just burst into tears again.

Finally, minutes later and with plenty of encouragement from him, I do end up telling him about the letter.

"Are you sure he didn't drop any hints? There was no indication at all last night that anything was bothering him at all?" Jase wonders out loud. Similar questions had been going through my mind ever since I reached home, to no avail.

"Nothing."

"Has he tried to contact you?"

"I don't know, I mean the phone rang earlier but I didn't check who it was. You're lucky I picked up just now," I say.

"From everything you've told me about the guy, this just seems bizarre. Completely out of character. He'd have to be a sociopath to hide all that from you!"

"That's what scared me, Jase! Either he's a brilliant liar, or I'm way more gullible than I thought. Either way, I'm fucked." Tears start to flow more heavily again.

"I don't know what to do. Only yesterday I would've done anything for him... I know this sounds utterly stupid, clearly I have no clue who he really is."

"Keep it together, Cath. You'll be fine, eventually. You'll land on your feet no matter what life throws at you."

"I loved him! Or who I thought he was anyway. It fucking hurts, way worse than with Greg, I just didn't see this coming at all..." My nose is leaking uncontrollably, causing me to sniffle.

"You're one of the most sensible people I know. Take your time to think it all over and if he gets in touch and you're up for it, even hear his side of things if you like. You'll realize you're doing the right thing."

"Yeah, I guess. Thanks," I say.

"Any time. Now you get out of the damn tub, wear something fabulous and stock up on whatever variety of Haagen-Dazs you deem appropriate. And don't you forget what an absolute catch you are! If anyone has lost out here, it's him."

The mental image of me strolling down to the shops to buy ice cream in the type of outfit Jase would pick out for me does amuse me, if only slightly.

When I hang up, I realize he's very right about one thing: I need to get out of this tub before my skin dissolves. And then... well, I'm not ready to face the outside world like this. Puffy eyelids, red eyes and a drippy colored nose. *No way.*

Instead I wear something fleecy and comfortable and carry my duvet with me to the sofa. Perhaps I'll watch some TV, but instead I sit motionless and stare at the black screen. I'm still dissecting and analyzing everything that's happened since yesterday afternoon. Above all, I feel utterly alone.

But I can't quite focus on the helpful things that would give me confidence in my choice to leave; the letter, the lie, his implied accusation about my absence when he reached work yesterday. These things fade away when I remember how vulnerable he looked when he said he'd be lost without me. Was that just an act?

I insisted that I wouldn't change my mind about him or leave. And yet that's exactly what I've done.

Did I have a choice, though? If only he'd told me everything from the start, I might not have been this upset. I might have forgiven everything and let it go, especially since his letter read like he tried to do the right thing, and left as soon as he realized what had happened. Instead he tricked me into making big commitments and promises, and still kept his dirty secret.

Then I think back to the moment here in my living room when he realized that I liked him as well. How shocked he looked when I told him.

It feels like forever ago and so much has happened since. We've moved way too fast, probably because of all that we'd fantasized about for weeks beforehand. We were both playing catch up with our bodies, because our minds were well ahead of reality.

Did I fall for *him*, or my fantasy of him?

I vividly recall all the ways he'd look at me lately; with affection, warmth, desire. I thought I'd seen love in his eyes. How could he fake all that?

How about protective John; when he saved me from Dick and felt so guilty for letting me go into his office alone. Was he only acting then too?

I mentally go through every event, every conversation, and it just confuses me further.

And then his letter, so weird and disjointed. It hardly made sense, as if he was quite drunk when he wrote it. Yet he specifically wrote about his sensible choices.

Now that I've had time to think, a lot of it doesn't add up. If he was indeed trying not to get drunk by opting for soft drinks instead, how come things got so out of hand anyway? Could he not control himself? Is he one of those people whose personality changes completely once they've had a couple of drinks?

And what bothers me even more is the tone of the letter. So remorseful, so deeply sad. It was the exact opposite of his carefree mood last night. Which was the act and which was truth? If you take out the bizarre and troubling events he outlines, what remains is a tragic declaration of his love for me. How could a drunk weave such an elaborate tale together and fabricate all that lovey-dovey stuff?

What if it wasn't fabricated?

My phone rings again. Seeing his name on the screen breaks me in half.

I want things to go back to how they were. But that's impossible. And if I answer the call, I won't be able to do much but blubber incoherently, so I pass on it.

Minute after minute passes and I'm still sitting there, legs pulled up against my chest with one arm around them. The phone in my other hand has since gone on stand-by.

A knock on the door startles me. I'm completely unprepared for what I hear next.

IX. JOHN

"Cath, are you in there?" I say, my voice sounding as shaky as I feel.

Please, please be home!

I knock again, louder this time and then rest my head against the door. There's no sign of movement inside. Complete silence.

Dialling her number again, I hope and pray that this time she answers. My heart is pounding my throat and I'm certain I won't be able to get a word out if she does pick up. I hear the faint sound of her phone through the door. She doesn't answer.

I try hitting my fist against the door once more. As if hoping and wishing hard enough could make her magically appear in front of me.

"Please, if you're home, let me in."

The only response I get is from the flat next door, a raspy female voice yells at me to piss off as I'm clearly wasting my time. Indeed. I expect that nothing I could do or say will sway her to forgive me, but I have to try to at least apologize or explain.

Her note from earlier was pretty clear, though unnecessary.

Had she only left the pad without any additions, I would've understood everything just as clearly.

The lengthy letter to her in my own handwriting shocked me for two reasons: firstly, the content, secondly that I don't remember any of it. Not the strip club, especially not the private show and having some random girl touch me *down there*. I have no recollection of how I got back to my hotel, never mind writing it all down. All I know is, I found the updated flight details in my email that morning and I never questioned who rebooked it.

She thinks I'm a monster and I can't blame her. How on earth did I get so wasted that I can't remember what happened? My last memories are from the nightclub, but anything after that is just gone. Blank.

When I woke up yesterday, I felt hungover. My head was fuzzy and achy and I couldn't remember how I got back the night before. I assumed that I'd drunk more than I thought. It scared me how miserably I had failed to stick to my plan of quitting after a few rounds. After promising her on Tuesday that I'd stop all that.

I was ashamed of my lack of self control or even my awareness of how it happened.

Had I found the pad yesterday, I wouldn't have been able to hide it; the guilt would've been written on my face. That's the one thing I want to explain to her, even if she won't want to hear it. I didn't try to deceive her. She deserves the truth; however horrible it is.

If she's not home now, I'm sure she'll have to come back at some point. With my back against the wall, I lower myself and sit down on the cold tiles outside her door.

At least two hours pass and nothing happens except the occasional door opening and closing and footsteps further down the hall. None of Cath's neighbors think to look around and my presence goes completely unnoticed.

Another half hour later my rambling thoughts are interrupted with a louder click and a rush of air right beside me. I rush to my feet and promptly forget everything I had planned to say to her.

"Oh!" Cath exclaims.

I have to remind myself to breathe but it's not working. She's frozen in front of me and I hardly dare to look her in the eye. It's obvious that she's been crying, a lot.

Her lips are pressed together tightly and she seems to be holding her breath. She avoids eye contact similarly but I can make out that her eyelashes are still wet.

If I don't break the silence now...

"You must think I'm a terrible person," I say, finally.

She looks up at me, frowning. Waiting.

"I didn't know... I mean..." *Deep breaths, you can do this!*

I clear my throat and keep my eyes fixated on the ground. If I look at her again, I'll lose my train of thought completely.

"I don't remember much from that night, not even writing the letter. I know that sounds unlikely..." I glance in her direction and note that the creases on her forehead have deepened.

With a sigh, I realize I probably wouldn't have believed me either.

"How can you not remember all that?" Her voice sounds low, not quite a whisper but still very far from her normal self. I'm not sure what's worse, facing the reality that I've lost her, or seeing her heartbroken.

I shake my head in response.

"I am so sorry I've let you down." My own voice cracks noticeably. "I wasn't trying to hide anything; I didn't have a clue about any of it until I read the damn thing myself."

When I look at her again, I see tears flooding her face. I wish I knew how to fix this; she doesn't deserve to be so hurt. I'm responsible; I should pay the price, not her. Before I know it, I can feel the stinging start in my own eyes.

"I don't know what to believe anymore." She stares at me with those mysterious eyes of hers. The sadness they reflect tugs at my insides until I can barely stand it.

"Believe whatever feels right. I don't know."

Just when I've lost every shred of hope, she takes a step back inside and nods at me to come in. The whole thing reminds me of another set of fairly unreliable and blurry memories I have, when I came here after finding her note. It's a strange kind of justice to find myself in the same place as our beginning, while facing our end.

"Tell me exactly what happened that night. Just what you *do* remember," she says.

I do as asked. I tell her about leaving the trade show venue around six, the bar, the night club. I distinctly remember the others were flirting with girls there, dancing and making fools of themselves. I remember feeling tipsy when I decided to stop drinking. And then everything turns black and I'm lost for words. The next thing I know, I get a wake up call from reception and find myself back in my room with an unexplained hangover.

With arms folded in front of her and a thoughtful look on her face, she restlessly shifts her weight back and forth from one leg to the other. Then she takes a few steps around the sofa and sits down with her back towards me. I'm not sure whether to follow her example or not, so I do nothing at all.

"I have spent the better part of today trying to convince myself that I'd been played. That if you could lie about something so significant, I could not be sure of how much else was fake as well," she says.

"I would never lie to you. None of it makes sense to me. I don't even look at other women, never mind paying a complete stranger to—" The thought alone makes me feel sick.

She turns around and studies my expression. Then her face relaxes and she pats the sofa beside her. I try to tell myself not to get my hopes up, but my heart starts to race anyway. Either way I'm glad to join her.

But when I do sit down, she starts to cry again, and helpless doesn't even begin to describe how I feel. She pulls her legs up in front of her and wraps her arms around them, hiding her face while her shoulders continue to shudder.

"Cath," I say. "Please don't."

"I believe you," she says and her sobs intensify.

Perhaps I should do something to console her, but it seems alien and uncomfortable. Like I'd be crossing an invisible boundary.

Eventually I do put my hand on her shoulder and I take it as a positive sign that she does not shake it off.

"Then why are you still crying?"

"Because I don't know how to take this back!"

"I don't understand," I say.

She leans against my hand and I'm encouraged to start caressing her shoulder. It feels nice to touch her again. Like I'm starting to bridge the huge gap between us.

"After finding something like that, rather than ask you about it, I just left." She looks up, her eyes full of remorse. "I didn't even give you a chance!"

I swallow hard and move in closer, putting my other arm around her too. She seems so fragile. More so than every other time I've held her. As if one mistake, one wrong move could break her in half. I remember everything she told me on the phone about her past.

She puts on a brave front, but she's been deeply wounded before. If she'll let me, I'll try my best to care for her for the rest of our lives.

"Had the tables been turned, I would've handled things much worse," I say.

"But don't you see... I went back on every promise, every commitment I'd made. It's inexcusable!"

"Okay, stop. That's nonsense. You're the best thing that's ever happened to me. All this stuff is secondary," I say.

"I'm so very sorry... " She rests her forehead into the crook of my neck and I try to hold her more tightly but due to the awkward angle, I decide to just lift her into my lap instead. Safely tucked into my arms, she noticeably calms down.

"I don't know what to do without you. I'll spend my whole life earning your forgiveness," I say.

The last of her tears transfer onto my skin, making me slightly itchy but I dare not move for fear of disturbing her. I don't want this moment to end, in case it's the last one like it.

I'm so relieved to have her in my arms. Don't know what I would've done had she not opened the door when she did. Probably I would've sat there in the hallway all day and perhaps all night, just waiting and thinking about how it all went wrong.

And to think I very nearly didn't dare to come over at all... Best not to consider what might've happened then.

"I love you," I whisper. "Never ever forget it."

She starts to plant soft, ticklish kisses below my ear. Although I still feel raw and wrung out, these small affections from her cause an intense reaction in me. My heartbeat is all over the place and my chest feels like it might burst open.

When she presses up against me and raises her head to nibble on my lips, I realize that more than the words that came before, this is our real reconciliation. I pour everything I have into our kiss and embarrassingly tear up yet again.

Her eyes widen when she sees, but she doesn't stop. Instead she holds my face in her hands, wiping the wetness off me with her thumbs, and lets her tongue respond to mine. She takes my breath away, replacing some of my earlier pain with a pressing need for her. One which of course she notices straight away, as she's sitting right on top of its most obvious indicator.

I let my feelings and her responses guide me, and try not to over analyze for a change. It feels right when I caress her hair, her back, down her sides and over her hips and back up again. It also feels right when she grinds down into my crotch and sends jolts of bittersweet pleasure through me.

But before I get too distracted, I just want to show her how special she is to me. So, I gather her up in my arms again, struggling but managing to get up somehow while still mid-kiss, and head to the bedroom. There is something very important I've so far failed to do. Something to show her that she's the most important person on earth. A goddess who deserves to be worshipped; I want to be worthy of her forgiveness.

Upon laying her down, I start to remove her pajamas. She leans up on her elbows, watching me. I kneel in between her legs, but that doesn't work so I lie down instead, propping myself up on my elbows. Now I'm able to reach and kiss her inner thighs.

"Will you accept this poor attempt at an apology?" I ask.

She nods and continues to watch me go further up the silky skin of her thighs, alternating between sides. Her body reacts instantly, muscles fluttering, back arching just a bit with each kiss. The scent of her arousal is intoxicating. So sweet and kind of floral as well. I run my finger over her, down her lips and in between to find a pool of moisture waiting for me.

Encouraged by her soft moans, I lean in and kiss her. Then I spread her open with my hand and kiss again, this time finding her clit to softly lick. She tastes wonderful, a hint of saltiness contrasting with the sweetness of her scent. I had been nervous about this before, another first to be tried with her. It turns out I had nothing to worry about.

X.

How could I be so idiotic, so paranoid that I completely lost any semblance of sanity and nearly ruined everything we had together? Of course, he didn't lie. There was another explanation for it all. I couldn't find any hint of dishonesty in his eyes, only truth and mostly fear.

I believe every word he said. If that's wrong and naive, then so be it. This connection which we share is worth taking a risk on.

I want us to be real. I want to *feel* again.

My mind goes blank, all negative thoughts banished by the onslaught of pleasure he's unleashing between my thighs. I can't control my moans, I don't want to either. He deserves to hear exactly what he's doing to me.

"Tell me how you like it," he says, pausing only for a moment before continuing to lick at my clit.

It makes me squirm, so intense is the sensation. I want more.

"It's perfect, keep going," I gasp.

He licks all around my outer, inner labia and further inwards. I am feverish and my muscles twitch almost uncontrollably. It takes a whole lot of control for me not to crush his head between my thighs.

A few more spasms later, he gets the hint and holds me firmly spread with both hands while fucking me with his tongue. It's beautiful, not just the pleasure he's giving

247

me but also the visual aspect. The way he looks up at me with wide eyes every so often.

He takes my clit between his lips again, gently sucks on it and slips a finger inside me. I buck my hips. I'm about to lose all control.

"Stop," I cry out. "Stop, stop, stop!"

He releases me with a startled frown. I smile at him and reach for his hand, pulling him further up the bed. At the same time, I crawl around until my head is nearer the foot end of the bed and unbutton his jeans, tugging impatiently.

As soon as he's got them off, I lie down on my side and wait for him to put his head on my thigh. Then I lean up onto my elbow and lick a droplet of pre-cum from his cock.

He groans into my crotch and tries to continue licking, sucking and fingering me from this new direction. I take his length into my mouth as far as it will go, and wrap my free arm around his thigh to steady myself. It's like a competition to see who distracts the other more. We're about equally matched.

Every time he flicks his tongue across my most sensitive parts, I moan uncontrollably with my mouth still full. Then I suck him harder, out and in until it won't go any further and he groans in response.

His finger moves inside me. When he finds my G-spot, heat and tension build to unmentionable levels. I am out of breath and weak, forced to merely hold on to him while he continues to probe me. Moving my hips to help him on his way, I squeeze my hand around his cock. He reacts with a shudder that goes through his hips and thighs.

Continuing to lick and suck on the outside, with first one and then two fingers in me, he pushes me along to the inevitable. I cry out, my hips twitching and squirming despite his firm grip on me as he tops it all off with more flicks from his tongue. He's a natural; able to read the slightest moan or shudder to decipher exactly what pleases me most.

My thigh goes limp and almost hits him in the face before his hand props it back up. He has withdrawn his fingers and is now just licking me with long deliberate slurps. All the while I'm lost in a state of complete bliss.

Once I finally catch my breath, I put all my focus into returning the favour.

With one hand firmly gripping his shaft, I bob my head back and forth on him. His cock feels so tense, so ready. It's almost as if he's pulsating with anticipation. Feeling his balls with my other hand, I notice he's tensing up elsewhere too; back, thighs, ass. I force my hand between his thighs, caressing and then rubbing the skin just behind his balls. His formerly urgent breaths turn irregular throughout my explorations.

He obviously enjoys it, how he reacts more intensely now than when I was only sucking him off. I continue to massage as well as mouth-fuck him and it isn't long until his balls contract, his thighs go hard as planks and he shudders uncontrollably into my face.

His loud animalistic groans encourage me to continue as best I can despite my trapped hand, round and round, stimulating the sensitive skin of his perineum. All the while, I drain and swallow every last drop of cum until he is spent.

*I'm so sorry, for everything.*I promise myself I'll never make the same mistake again.

He reaches down, his hand trying but failing to get a grip around my shoulder. His hand finds my wrist, gently tugging until I turn right side up. Glad to be surrounded in a most perfect embrace again, I can feel a calm envelop us which makes everything almost feel okay again. The slow and relaxed kisses he plants on my cheek tell me he feels it too.

"Can I stay?" he asks.

There is no need to respond verbally, instead I hug him tightly and half-rid him of his T-shirt. He seems sufficiently reassured after I kiss his bare chest a couple of times because he sighs and rests his arm protectively around me.

"Let's promise each other that no matter what happens—whatever suspicions we may have, or rumours we've heard—we'll always hear each other out?" I ask.

He caresses my back, slipping his hands in under my top, and kisses my hair.

"Sounds like a plan," he says, "I just need to know one thing…"

"What's that?"

"Aren't you upset at all about what I did in Germany? Because I am," he says.

I shrug and think for a bit. "To be honest, I haven't

really considered it. I was too busy focussing on whether or not you'd lied to me."

Even now, I can't really wrap my head around it. It's too surreal, too out of character. I've seen him drunk before, and he didn't behave too strangely even then. I don't believe alcohol changes a person; it just unleashes their true selves. There's something else at play... As if he'd been drugged somehow.

For a few minutes, neither of us says a word.

"I'm so sorry I doubted you," I whisper finally.

He runs his fingers through my hair, sending goose bumps down my spine.

"And I'm sorry I let things get out of hand," he says. "It'll never happen again. Promise."

Our moment of quiet reflection is loudly interrupted by my stomach, which has decided that enough is enough. As soon as it stops growling, he pokes me softly in the side.

"Don't tell me you haven't eaten all day?"

I shrug. "Wasn't hungry."

"Then allow me to change that..." He gets up and starts to put on his jeans while I watch from the comfort of the warm bed.

I decide to follow him into the kitchen after a few moments, partially because I'm curious to see what he's up to, but mainly because I can't bear the thought of being apart right now. Not while our wounds are still raw.

I find him rummaging through the fridge, looking for God knows what, before laying out all the vital components of ham and cheese sandwiches on the counter.

"Have you got a sandwich toaster?" he asks.

I nod and find it for him, then stand back and look on as he assembles the ingredients.

I get it now. Why he continued to watch me when I cooked for him. It's a lovely thing, observing that special someone busy at work. I could do this for hours.

My stomach claws at my insides violently again when the aroma of golden toasties fills the room. I get the plates and as soon as they're ready we sit down to eat around the breakfast bar. The envelope that came in the mail yesterday is still lying there so I mindlessly open it while taking a few bites.

"Goddamnit, I can't fucking believe this!" I drop the half-eaten sandwich back into the plate and grab the letter with both, reading it in depth again.

"What happened?" John asks.

"I'm being evicted! My landlord has given me a month's notice starting yesterday. Some building refurbishment planned for the New Year it says. I can bet he's just trying to get rid of me to up the rent!"

My appetite is ruined and all the rawness from earlier in the day flares up again. It's always something. One thing gets better, another fucks up. I feel like Lady Luck is torturing me on purpose, sending me on an emotional rollercoaster and making bits of track disappear underneath me without warning. I drop the letter onto the table.

John picks it up to read it for himself.

With my head in both hands, I try to think. What do I do, how will I find a new place at such short notice?

"You've got a month, surely that's enough time to figure out something?" he asks.

He reaches across the bar and starts to caress my shoulder.

"If he doesn't give me my deposit back early, I literally can't afford it!" My throat feels tight and I'm developing a splitting headache again.

"And plus, it's almost Christmas. Who the hell is going to conduct viewings over the holiday period? The timing couldn't have been worse," I complain.

He puts the letter down and gets up, then within seconds he stops beside me and puts his arms around me once more.

I'm too emotionally drained after everything for further tears, so I just sit there, frozen in his embrace. What I need is a sensible plan.

I've got nothing.

"You know, today has made me think really hard about everything," he says. "I couldn't face the thought of having to live without you. I realised that—"

I'm only half listening to him, mostly preoccupied with trying to force my mind into trouble-shooting mode. *There must be something I can do?*

He clears his throat, causing me to snap out of my moment of self-pity and look up at him.

"It's not sensible, or rational and of course much too soon... But I need you in my life, Cath. I can't think of anything better than to spend my evenings with you, my nights holding you in my arms. So..." he rambles on.

I blink a few times, trying to let his words filter through the clutter in my brain.

What is he trying to say?

"You could stay with me, if you like. Just for a while, until you find a new place if you need your space. Or... You know, just stay."

He looks concerned. No, that's an understatement. He looks terrified.

And I don't know how to respond. Does he really mean it? Then again, if not, why would he suggest it? Is this just his guilt about the business trip talking?

"Are you sure?" I ask.

I'm worried as well, hoping that his offer is genuine, and not coerced. It sounds too good to be true.

He forces an awkward smile. "I won't lie, I'm about ready to crap my pants right now."

"Because I might say no? Or because I might say yes?" I ask.

He averts his gaze from me, and hesitates for a moment.

"A bit of both... It's just that I've been here before, in a similar situation. And although I want to make it perfectly clear that you're nothing like her it's still a bit weird. Scary."

Indeed, she really did a number on him. It still makes me angry just thinking about it.

"I don't want to make you uncomfortable," I say.

"No, no, no." He shakes his head and looks at me again. "That's not what I meant. I just wanted to explain myself. My offer stands. I would love to spend every day and night with you."

Continuing to look at me, he anxiously awaits my answer while I try to make sense of it all. I also can't imagine my life without him now. After our reconciliation, I'm even more mindful of how strong my feelings for him are. Is there a downside to accepting?

My mind has let me down once already today, causing nothing but pain when my heart wanted to continue to believe in us. It's obvious which to follow on this.

I slip my hands around his neck and pull him close to me.

"Yes. I'd love to move in with you. But if you ever change your mind..."

"I told you already, I could never lie to you. If I don't think it's working out, I'll say so. Promise me you'll do the same?" he asks.

I nuzzle against the side of his face. My heart races with some amount of fear but mainly excitement. He leans back and kisses me on the lips.

"I promise," I whisper, before returning his kiss with a less innocent one.

When I see his eyes flash open in front of me, I know. It'll all work out somehow.

What we have together is special. A once-in-a-lifetime thing.

Rational or not, I'm ready to take this chance.

Together.

AUTHOR'S NOTE

Thanks for reading *Just Another Day at the Office*! Whether this is your first experience of my work, or you've been with me from the early days, I appreciate every one of you.

This story dates from 2013, when it was first released as a serialised novel. It was one of the first things I ever published back when I was still writing under my old pen name, "Hedonist Six" and it has informed much of my work ever since.

Since 2016 I've been planning to rework it into the book it always deserved to be, but always kept putting it off. I've grown as a writer over the years, so it's only obvious that this-my debut novel-started out flawed. I was worried that I'd hate the experience of rewriting it. That I'd spend the whole time cringing at all the mistakes I'd made and lose confidence in my abilities as an author.
But when I picked it up finally during the summer of 2019, I found that my concerns were largely unfounded. Awkward language is easy to fix, as long as the story is mostly there.

I fell in love with the characters all over again and became swept up in their whirlwind romance. Cath and John are special to me. These are the characters I have spent the most time with, in more ways than just one. I fancy myself mostly a novella writer. At around 57,000 words, this is my longest book to date. Along with it being one of my oldest works, I do feel like I've known these two characters for years.

It has always been my aim to be as honest as possible in my stories. Not everyone fits into the same mould. And not everyone is attracted to the same things. When I first wrote this story, it was the romance that I personally wanted to read but could not find on the shelves. I didn't want a dominant romance hero with six pack abs, I wanted to see the sort of guy who had been largely ignored in fiction. A regular guy with regular hang-ups and insecurities. By now, I have a sizeable catalogue of similarly themed stories out.

Cath, meanwhile, is a younger version of me in some ways. I've given her a more tragic back story than my own, but that's about it. I relate to her insecurities and especially her tendency to give up all of herself for love. I also relate to her physical preferences when it comes to men. I think a lot of women can appreciate a big cuddly man, even if they don't always say so out loud.

In this book we follow Cath's journey of love at first sight initially. Although weeks pass before she makes her first move, she gives it her all and loses herself to John immediately. We find out the feeling was mutual all along and they were both just too messed up to do anything about it right away.

I can relate to this feeling very well. When my husband and I first got together it was after a friendship that had already lasted for a few months. But once we realised that we could become more than friends, we fell hard and fast. We knew we wanted to spend our lives together only days into our affair. This kind of passion is what I aim to create in a lot of my books.

So, I hope you enjoyed the journey as much as I have and that perhaps you'll be tempted to read more of my work. Do take a look at the other dad bod romances I have written and published.

Love, Lorelei

- ❖ Lmoone.com
- ❖ Lorelei Moone on Facebook

By the way, I also write Paranormal Romance as Lorelei Moone. If that's also your cup of tea, then please take a look at loreleimoone.com.

www.ingramcontent.com/pod-product-compliance
Lightning Source LLC
Chambersburg PA
CBHW070621170726
48291CB00003B/822